In or... ...ent
he stopped her flight

"Where the devil have you been?" He sounded infuriated, almost beyond knowing what he was saying. "You think it's your mission in life to make me suffer?" he snarled.

His face was icy and barbaric. Helen stared at him as he spun her fully round to face him, his eyes annihilating her. "Stein?" she breathed weakly, as he forced her to look at him. She wasn't sure what to make of his livid accusation, but she was astonished at the anger in his face.

He drew a deep breath between his teeth and, snatching her up in his arms, carried her straight into his study. As she was held tightly against him, her heartbeats quickened, and she felt as if she was going to choke.

She tried desperately to hang on to her deserting senses....

Books by Margaret Pargeter

These books may be available at your local bookseller.

For a free catalog listing all titles currently available,
send your name and address to:

Harlequin Reader Service
2504 West Southern Avenue, Tempe, AZ 85282
Canadian address: Stratford, Ontario N5A 6W2

MARGARET PARGETER

chains of regret

Harlequin Books

TORONTO • NEW YORK • LONDON
AMSTERDAM • PARIS • SYDNEY • HAMBURG
STOCKHOLM • ATHENS • TOKYO • MILAN

Harlequin Presents first edition December 1983
ISBN 0-373-10653-X

Original hardcover edition published in 1983
by Mills & Boon Limited

CHAPTER ONE

THE plane gave a slight bump as planes usually do when they land. Helen tried to relax in her seat until it came to a stop, but found it impossible. Inside she was too tensed up. With the other passengers she left the plane and went through the customary routine, breathing a sigh of relief when finally she was free to look round for her father.

Anxiously she searched the milling crowds. He had to be somewhere. She had sent two cables, one to Oakfield, one to his office here in London, telling him the exact time and date of her arrival, so he must know she was coming. It had been over a year since she had seen him, but in his letters he had always said how delighted he would be to have her home again. Had he meant it? she wondered uneasily when he didn't appear. She couldn't remember him ever keeping her waiting like this.

Then, to her dismay, she saw his partner, Stein Maddison, striding towards her, as usual looking as though he was capable of ruling the world. Her face paling, Helen almost turned and ran, but before she could move he was standing directly in front of her. Her heart beating unsteadily, she realised she had left it too late.

As though he guessed she would have liked to escape and meant to make sure she didn't, Stein swiftly took hold of her arm. 'Hello, Helen,' he said quietly.

His voice was so soft, Helen wondered why she should think of a cobra ready to strike. 'Hello, Stein,' she replied, forcing a smile, clamping down on her turbulent emotions. Hadn't she resolved in France to get rid of her old antagonism? It had never done her

5

any good, and by running away she must have played right into Stein's hands. He must have been glad to see the last of her, especially after their last quarrel, when she had told him exactly how much she despised him.

His grey eyes were going coolly over her, something in their grey depth making her flinch, but he only observed mildly, 'So you decided to come home at last?'

Helen flushed unhappily. 'Perhaps I shouldn't have stayed away so long.'

'Perhaps you shouldn't,' he agreed tautly.

Helen wished he wasn't so tall and broad. Somehow Stein had always managed to make her feel small and defenceless, even when he was being nice to her. 'I didn't really intend staying away at all,' she whispered.

Stein didn't appear to hear her remorseful tones. 'Time usually passes swiftly when one's enjoying oneself,' he observed sarcastically.

'I . . .' She began to say she had been working, not enjoying herself, then decided against it. He wouldn't believe her—and she didn't blame him. Instead she said, 'I expected to see my father. Where is he?'

There was a slight pause while Stein's steely fingers bit into her arm, and with a murmur of painful protest Helen glanced up at him. She was shocked to see a certain whiteness around his mouth.

'Stein?' she exclaimed.

'He's at Oakfield,' he answered shortly, picking up her suitcase and propelling her over the tarmac. 'We should be there within the hour.'

He was driving himself and she settled in the powerful Rolls with a sigh of relief. 'Business must be booming,' she patted the luxurious upholstery lightly, 'when we can still afford cars like this!'

'Yes,' he said curtly, concentrating on leaving the airport.

Helen sighed. She had merely been trying to lighten the atmosphere and had hoped he would at least meet her halfway. Glancing uncertainly at his rock-hard profile, she tried to stop feeling so strangely apprehensive.

'Is Dad all right?' she asked suddenly, wondering if this was the cause of Stein's grim face.

'I guess so,' he assured her briefly, yet she noticed he didn't relax an inch.

A taxi missed them by inches, then cut in front of them so that Stein had to slam on his brakes. They both jerked forward, their seatbelts holding, while Stein cursed under his breath. Helen decided not to ask any more questions until they were clear of the worst of the traffic.

Rather furtively, while his attention was engaged elsewhere, she studied him. Because she loved her father and Stein was the son he had always longed for, she had decided at last to accept him. It might not be easy to begin with, but if she apologised for the things she had said, surely he would be willing to bury the hatchet? He might be full of unforgiving pride, but if she suggested generously that they should begin again, she didn't see how he could refuse.

Helen's immediate surroundings faded as she recalled the day her father told her he was taking a partner. 'It's more of a merger really, Helen,' he had explained vaguely. 'Stein's a younger man with a formidable reputation in our line of business. We need him.'

Helen had felt stunned. 'I can't speak for Mr Maddison, Dad,' she had retorted scathingly, 'but we certainly don't need anyone!'

Lester Davis had shaken his grey head. 'I've been thinking of it for a long time and Stein's just the man I've been looking for. He's thirty-four and perhaps a shade too arrogant, but he knows what he wants and where he's going.'

'I'll tell him where he can go to if he dares show his face in here!' Helen had cried, with all the impulsive temper of her eighteen years.

'Don't be foolish, Helen,' Lester looked both startled

and uncomfortable. 'You'll soon get used to the idea, and it's not like you to be unreasonable. Besides, it's all settled. He starts next week, so it won't be necessary for you to come in any more. You can stay at Oakfield and learn how to run the house. It's been neglected long enough, ever since your mother died, when you were born.'

'Stay at home?' Helen sank into the chair at the other side of her father's desk, at last beginning to take him seriously. Was she going crazy, or was it everyone else? She had come to the firm straight from school and had only been working six months, but she'd been determined to learn everything so she could take over from her father one day. Now he was practically telling her he had no further use for her! Well, she wouldn't allow him to throw her out that easily! 'Whose idea is this?' she had asked coldly. 'Yours or Mr Maddison's?'

'Why, mine, of course,' Lester muttered, but she hadn't believed him. She guessed from his flushed, embarrassed face that he wasn't telling the truth.

Helen, clenching her hands, had stared at him. 'Don't you see,' she had exclaimed sharply, 'once I'm out of the way he might easily get rid of you as well. You need me here to keep an eye on him.'

'No!' Lester had interrupted hastily.

'I can't understand,' Helen raged suspiciously, 'why you've been so secretive. I know I agreed to start at the bottom, so I don't hear much about what's going on at your level, but you've never even asked me to meet him! You could surely have dropped a hint as to what you were thinking of doing?'

'You'd only have made a fuss,' Lester muttered.

'Haven't I the right?' she had asked in a strangled voice.

'Mr Maddison didn't want it made public,' Lester replied, his face stubborn, obviously having no idea how he was hurting his daughter.

Helen flinched. 'It will be now, though. So what did

you hope to achieve? Quite frankly, I don't like the sound of your Mr Maddison.'

'You'll like him!' Lester had looked unhappy but eager. 'He wants to meet you as soon as possible, now that everything's settled.'

Ignoring this, Helen had cried bitterly, 'I know you've always regretted I wasn't a boy, but you didn't have to push me out!'

'No one's pushing you out,' Lester had insisted with an impatient glance at Helen's white face. 'I think you'd be better at home, that's all. If only you'd be reasonable you'd soon see you were never cut out to be a business woman.'

Helen was twenty now and could still remember how wounded she had felt when her father said that, and she had hated Stein Maddison even before their first meeting.

When her father introduced them she tried to convince herself she had met plenty of men like him, but she knew this wasn't true. He was tall and powerfully built, with chiselled features and cool grey eyes. Dark hair topped a face that was hard and assertive. Helen's gaze had wandered apprehensively over the high cheekbones, his straight nose and firm but sensuous mouth. He was the kind of man who commanded attention, and she had suddenly shivered as his hard vitality struck her like a blow.

He had given no indication of being aware of her resentment as he smiled and held out his hand. Helen had hated feeling obliged to shake hands with him, and had hated even more the peculiar sensation which shot through her as her slim white fingers were engulfed by his. She had wanted to scream at him childishly and tell him to get out of their lives! It was only because of her father's pleading glance that she had held her tongue, but as soon as he had gone she had told Lester she would be glad to retire to Oakfield. She was convinced it wouldn't be long before Stein Maddison left and her father would be begging her to return.

Unfortunately Stein hadn't left. Within a month or two it became very obvious he was there to stay. Helen was further outraged when her father began bringing him home for dinner and inviting him to stay for weekends. He even set aside a suite of rooms on the first floor and assured Stein he was welcome to use them whenever he wished.

Helen was incensed. She had ignored Stein's friendly overtures, and when he asked her to go out with him she had refused. He hadn't given up trying, not straight away. He continued doing everything he could to please her, he had even begun bringing her flowers, which she had viewed with secret contempt and stuffed in the dustbin at the first opportunity. Despite his efforts she had remained cool and distant, making sure he understood that she would never demean herself by having anything more to do with him than was absolutely necessary.

The little she discovered about him merely added to her scorn and dislike. He apparently came from a very humble background and had worked his way up—by taking advantage of tired old men, she decided fiercely, and getting rid of their daughters! Not until Stein kissed her one evening did it suddenly occur to her that far from getting rid of her he might, incredibly, be hoping to marry her, so that he would get everything when her father died.

When Stein · had kissed her Helen had been so terrified by the flame of response inside her that she was ready to believe anything. As with a smothered groan his arms had tightened around her slender young body, she had pushed him frantically away. Furiously she had slapped his face then turned and run, vowing never to let him near her again.

After this Helen had given up all pretence of trying to comply with her father's wishes. Because she had never been truly ambitious she had settled down quite well at

Oakfield. She might not have done much work, but she had squandered her time fairly innocently. If it hadn't been for Stein Maddison's disruptive presence and his increasing pursuit of her, she might have been content.

From the moment he kissed her she began feeling irrationally threatened. Fearing she might not be able to resist him, should he choose to exert any pressure, to avoid him she had begun going frequently to London. She had stayed with friends and attended wild parties. By sheer coincidence he had turned up at one of these and rescued her from an assault by a drunken youth. Stein's silence had been strangely explosive as he had practically dragged her from the house back to Oakfield, while, far from being grateful, she had called him all the names she could lay tongue to.

Helen swallowed a wave of shame as she recalled some of the things she had said.

'You're nothing but a nobody, out for what he can get!' she had shouted, wiping hysterical tears from her eyes, 'You don't fool me as you've managed to fool my father! I know you're being nice to me because you'd like to get your hands on his money!'

Lifting her from his car, Stein had frowned darkly down on her distraught young face, noting the beauty which neither tears nor temper could mar. 'You're quite wrong——' he had begun.

'I'd never marry you!' she had interrupted furiously.

'Wait until you're asked,' he had retorted less gently.

'I hate you!' she cried, strung up beyond reason, as she usually was when she got too near him. 'I hate my father, too, for having anything to do with you. I'll make you both regret the day he took you into the firm!'

'Helen!' Stein had let her slide to the ground very slowly, while still holding her closely. 'Please, darling, don't!' he had groaned. 'Your father . . .'

Again she had cut him off. 'Don't talk to me about my father!' she gasped, despising him for grovelling as she wrenched herself free. 'You can both go to hell for all I care!'

The next day she had fled to France and stayed with an old school friend. No one would miss her, she felt sure. Her father had Stein now to look after his interests, and Stein had only tried to cultivate her friendship in order to gain by it. For a while she didn't let either of them know where she was.

When Helen had been at school she had spent several holidays with her friend Fawn Sommier and her parents, who had always welcomed her. They had a charming house in the South of France and appeared to be quite affluent. Since her last visit, however, much had changed. Fawn's father had died and her mother, an Englishwoman by birth, had told Helen that, much as she loved having her she could no longer afford to keep her for nothing. Her circumstances were, alas, sadly changed.

Immediately, with her usual impulsiveness, Helen had written and asked her father to send her a substantial sum. She hadn't said why she required it, but when it arrived she had given it all to Madame Sommier, who, believing Lester Davis to be wealthy, had greedily taken every penny.

Helen had been in France only two weeks when a neighbour's husband, a distant relative of the Sommiers, was killed in a road accident. Because she had felt desperately sorry for the young widow, and no one else seemed inclined to help, Helen offered to look after the house and her three children while Madame Sibour took over the running of the family vineyard.

She had stayed almost a year, during which she had learnt that her own troubles were nothing compared with those Raissa Sibour faced and eventually conquered. The children were darlings, and she soon came to love them and didn't mind the hard work. To work until she was too tired to think seemed the only way to counteract the feelings of guilt she experienced whenever she thought of Stein and her father. She often thought with great longing of her father, but although he wrote regularly she could never bring herself to reply to his letters. Nothing had changed at Oakfield, she gleaned. The firm was expanding and Stein was still there, but after her wild behaviour and the way she had left, she could never find the courage to go back.

When she did decide to go home again it happened so suddenly that she was in Paris, sending word to her father, almost before she realised what she was doing. In the space of a month Raissa Sibour had fallen in love and remarried, and Helen had felt it was time to move on. She'd had very little money as Fawn's mother had kept everything she had given her and she had refused to take wages from Madame Sibour. She had just enough to keep herself in Paris for a week before leaving for London.

Helen hadn't realised how homesick she had been until they left the city behind and her eyes rested once more on the green fields of England. She could scarcely believe she had stayed away as long, neglecting those she loved most. Without pausing to dissect such a thought, she turned contritely to the man by her side.

'Stein,' she laid a humble hand on his arm, attempting to convey her desire to forget the past and make amends, 'I'm sorry if I didn't seem pleased to see you at the airport.' Her voice faltered as he jerked his arm away. She turned her head and shrank back in her seat. His face looked harder than ever and a tiny nerve jerked by the side of his mouth. Was her touch so distasteful? This was the first time she had ever touched him voluntarily. She had behaved badly when she had first known him, but she had been young. In the year she had been away she had grown considerably older. Surely he could understand?

Uneasily she stirred under his long, calculating stare. 'So?' he prompted harshly.

She stiffened, muttering with a hint of her old

rebelliousness, 'Nothing. That is,' she glanced at him again, her blue eyes unconsciously appealing, 'I'm just trying to apologise. It was good of you to come and meet me. I do appreciate it.'

'Prove it!'

With a speed to match the snapping briefness of his terse command, he drew swiftly off the road. The shady layby might have been made for him. Before Helen had time to realise what was happening, he was pulling her roughly into his arms, kissing her deeply.

He swung her against him, crushing her mouth with his, cutting off her cry of protest. Too surprised by his action to resist immediately, Helen began experiencing almost forgotten sensations. The heat and weakness she had known vaguely before when he had kissed her returned, making her feel helpless. Despite the painful tightness of his arms, she began floating as his lips assaulted hers in a way she found both devastating and exciting.

It was nothing like his previous kisses. Pressed hard against him, she felt the demands of his body, commanding and receiving her response. She found it impossible to struggle against the authority and expertise he was wielding, and blindly she surrendered to both. Unable to combat the turbulence inside her, she clung to him, her arms sliding around his neck, her fingers threading convulsively through the thick darkness of his hair. Her eyes closed heavily as her ability to resist him disappeared and her body yielded to his caressing hands.

After long moments he released her and she stared at him mutely, eyes wide with confusion. He drew back, but not before she caught the gleam of harsh satisfaction on his face—and something else which seemed to cancel out any warmth. Helen wasn't sure what it was, but it filled her with the same nameless apprehension she had felt at the airport.

'Stein,' she swallowed nervously, while attempting to

hide a sudden shudder, 'hadn't we better get on?'

'Yes.' He removed his glance from her throbbing lips, his eyes glittering, but stayed right where he was.

Helen knew suddenly there was something terribly wrong. 'Please,' she whispered, trying to control incomprehensible panic, 'can't we go now? Dad must be waiting. If we don't turn up soon he'll be anxious.'

'He won't ever be anxious again,' he smiled.

His smile shook her. There was no humour in it, it was merely a savage twist of his lips and his eyes held hate. 'What do you mean?' she shivered.

He didn't flicker an eyelid and there was ice in his face. 'Your father died at the beginning of the week, Helen. His funeral's tomorrow.'

Helen stared at him, her eyes slowly dilating and darkening with shock. Every bit of colour fled from her face as if wiped off by a sponge. A terrible terror gripped her and she tried to stop herself shaking. Stein couldn't be serious, but didn't he realise what he was saying?

Frantically she sought for breath, her voice breaking. 'You're joking!' she gasped. 'You're trying to punish me by being deliberately cruel!'

'It's coming quite natually,' he taunted, his glance without sympathy on her grey, pinched face. Grimly he added, 'You don't have to believe me. You'll soon see for yourself.'

Helen tried to fight the harsh sickness rising in her throat. 'Then you aren't joking?'

'No,' curtly Stein ignored her shocked, beseeching expression. 'He had a heart attack.'

The extreme coldness of his voice chilled her. 'When?'

'A few days ago.' Suddenly he grasped her shoulders and began shaking her, as though he would really have liked to strangle her. 'We tried to contact you. He kept asking for you, but your friends the Sommiers could only tell me they believed you were in Paris, presumably enjoying yourself.'

'Stein!' Helen stared at him, her face contorted as a mounting horror ran through her veins. She wanted to ask more questions about her father, but Stein shook her so hard she was unable to speak. Her head was rolling on her shoulders and he seemed to have forgotten what he was doing as he viewed her with extreme loathing. As she attempted to wrench free of him, the pain from his hands merged with that which began piercing her heart. A dark cloud fell, obscuring his face, however hard she tried to focus. She strove to speak, her mouth working, she suspected distortedly, but she only managed an inarticulate little cry as her immediate surroundings faded and she sank unconscious against him.

Helen had always been fond of her bedroom at Oakfield and since her return home yesterday, it was the one place more than anywhere else where she wanted to be. She had never looked on it as a refuge before, but this was how she viewed it this afternoon, as she entered like a sleepwalker and closed the door.

Blindly she stared at the new black coat and hat which she had thrown numbly on her bed an hour earlier. Stein had bought them, they had been waiting for her. Did he intend them to be, she wondered wildly, a permanent reminder of her sins?

Steeped in misery, she turned away, ready to admit she deserved this and worse. When one of the departing mourners had commented fatuously that she would soon feel better, because life must go on, she had felt like screaming. How could she expect or even want to feel better, after what she had done?

Helplessly she sank in a chair by the window, trying to get a grip on herself. Although stunned by grief and remorse, she hadn't yet been able to weep, she had been too frozen inside. Now, as she felt tears threatening, she knew they were a luxury she couldn't afford, not until she had seen Stein. Soon she must go down and ask him if he intended staying on, and when she must see her father's lawyer. She had no particular wish for Stein to stay, but at the same time she didn't know how she was to get through the next few days without him.

Distractedly Helen thrust back the mane of tawny hair which, having escaped the neat coil at the back of her slender neck, insisted on falling over her face. She found it almost impossible to believe her father was gone, his funeral over. He had been laid to rest that afternoon in the small churchyard in the nearby village. The vicar, who had conducted the simple service, had been kind, but even he had been unable to disperse the feeling of unreality which had been with her ever since Stein had told her of her father's death.

Stein . . . In odd moments, when she stopped thinking of her father, Helen tried to fathom the bewildering pattern of his behaviour since he had met her yesterday at the airport. There were so many questions to which she couldn't find answers. Why, for instance, hadn't he told her immediately about her father? Why had he waited until he had kissed her? And why had he kissed her at all in such circumstances, and especially when he despised her?

Bitterly she reflected on his conduct this afternoon. No one, observing how carefully he had looked after her during the last few difficult hours, could have guessed his true feelings. He had been by her side, his hand under her arm, his eyes constantly on her pale face, ready with an encouraging word whenever she faltered. He had walked with her into the old stone-flagged church and out again, through the mud and rain, to the graveside. Back at Oakfield he had relieved her amost entirely of the burden and strain of coping with those who returned with them to the house for light refreshments. Despite the solemnity of the occasion, Helen had sensed many of the women envying her Stein's dark, immaculate presence.

They didn't realise, of course, how much he hated

her. She supposed she ought to be grateful that he had chosen to disguise it for even such a short space of time. In some ways she welcomed his derision as she felt she ought to suffer for neglecting her father. It was no excuse that she had considered that with a housekeeper and Stein, he would be well enough looked after. It was too late to try and absolve herself on these grounds. She ought to have come back to see him, or at least written more often.

Despairingly Helen dropped her head in her hands and sighed. Apart from the past, which she had no doubt would hurt for a long time to come, there was also the future to consider. There would be a lot of decisions to make, some of which must involve Stein. She would have to decide about things like whether to offer him her father's shares in the firm, or whether to keep hold of them herself.

Would it be possible, she wondered, to step into her father's shoes? She wasn't sure if she was capable of doing this, with her lack of experience, but perhaps Harold Dent, Lester's solicitor, could advise her. She would have Oakfield, but it was a huge, rambling old house, really far too big for one. It might probably be wiser to sell and get something smaller, even a flat in town, where she might find something to do. In country areas there was little employment and, even if she could afford it, especially after the past year, she was unable to contemplate a life of complete idleness.

When she was sure the last of the guests were gone, Helen rose reluctantly to her feet. She dared not risk Stein accusing her of shirking her responsibilities by remaining up here any longer. Once they were alone again she had little hope that his softer mood would continue, but the last thing she wanted to do was incite his anger. Running a quick comb through her tangled hair, but without checking otherwise that she was neat, she ran swiftly downstairs.

She didn't think Harold Dent had attended the

funeral, but she could have missed him. She hadn't seen
him in years as her father had rarely invited him to
Oakfield. He could be waiting now to deal with the
estate. Some solicitors preferred to get the reading of
the will over and done with as soon as possible.

The spacious lounge was deserted and she asked the
maid, busy clearing away, if she knew where she could
find Mr Maddison.

'He's in the library, miss.' The girl looked at her
curiously. She was new since a year ago, but Helen
hadn't noticed until this morning. There had been other
changes too while she had been away, which she hadn't
yet had the time or heart to go into. The staff at
Oakfield, in the past, had often changed. The house was
isolated, the nearest village beyond easy walking
distance, but their last housekeeper had been a nice
woman. Helen wondered what had happened to her.
The new one didn't seem nearly as pleasant.

She knocked on the library door like a guest.
Reminding herself that she wasn't one didn't help. Her
nerves were still strung too tight to allow her to behave
normally.

Stein was sitting behind her father's desk and glanced
up from the papers he was studying as she walked in.
Again Helen experienced a flicker of half forgotten
resentment that he should be making himself so much
at home. Angry with herself, she averted her face,
hoping she hadn't betrayed what she was thinking. She
had a sincere desire to be friends with Stein now, and it
amazed her how the antagonism she tried to forget kept
resurfacing.

'I imagined you'd be resting,' he said smoothly,
bringing her eyes back to him as he rose to his feet.
When she shook her head, he waved her to a chair.
'You look exhausted, you'd better sit down.'

'I couldn't rest.' Helen's voice choked as she
complied, but she rushed on before he could comment,
'I'd like to thank you for everything . . .'

'I was glad to be of help.'

She met the cool grey eyes, her own wide and anxious. 'I thought Mr Dent would be here. You know—my father's solicitor.'

'I know who he is.' Stein left the desk to stand near her before the fire. 'Didn't I mention it? He's on holiday and can't see you for another week.'

'A week?' Helen gazed at him uncertainly. 'It's a large firm, couldn't they have sent someone else?'

'Is there anything you're particularly worried about?' he asked curtly.

'No, it was silly of me. I got it into my head that Mr Dent would be here and you might be having to entertain him. In fact,' she stared at her clenched hands in her lap, 'I never heard Dad mention making a will, but I suppose he must have done.'

'I'm sure he left his affairs in order,' Stein returned formally.

Helen jumped up again quickly, as something in Stein's manner began affecting her oddly. There was a calculating glint in his eyes and she had a feeling he was deceiving her. Yet how could he be? They weren't discussing anything legal, and if she chose, she could easily check up on Mr Dent.

'Are you going back to town this evening?' she asked hastily.

'To town?' He searched her flushed face, his brows drawing together. 'No. Why should I?'

She bit her lip, wishing she could see a clear course to steer instead of having to stumble blindly. 'You've been staying here.'

His grey eyes went icy, but only for a moment. 'Your father was a lonely man.'

Did he have to keep rubbing it in? Helen nodded silently.

'Would you rather be on your own? I'll leave if you like?' he offered silkily.

'No, no, of course not,' Helen willed herself to speak

evenly. 'Stay as long as you like. I just wondered what your plans were.'

'Naturally.'

She heard the sardonic emphasis in his voice and wasn't sure what to say next. She had a feeling now that he was baiting her, but she was so tense that it was probably only her imagination working overtime. Stein might not be regarding her very kindly, but there was nothing in his eyes to suggest he was her enemy. If yesterday he hadn't been pleasant, it was understandable. He must have been upset because of her father, but, in the past, he had always forgiven her.

'There's bound to be a lot to see to,' she explained vaguely. 'I'll have to decide what to do about the business and—and everything, and I expect you'll have your problems too?'

He smiled gently, a smile which didn't quite reach his eyes. 'The year you've spent in Paris can't have prepared you for anything like this. You'll need advice.'

'Paris?' Helen's breath caught. 'Who told you I was there?'

'Madame Sommier. I was trying to find you, remember? She said you'd only been with her a week or two.' His voice hardened. 'Were you living with a man in Paris?'

'No!' she replied tightly, glaring at him. 'And I'm sure Madame Sommier didn't suggest I was.'

'She didn't suggest you weren't,' he returned her angry stare coolly. 'Some girls don't mind admitting they enjoy having affairs, but perhaps yours went wrong? Was that why you came home? Had you decided to try your luck again here?'

Stein was talking as though he was discussing the weather. His words held the animosity, not his voice. Suddenly Helen knew he had weapons and was going to use them, and that he also knew she couldn't fight back.

She shivered, her anger fading, her hands clenching and unclenching at her sides. Since her return she was seeing him differently from the image she had carried around with her for so long. She saw now that he was a handsome, even striking-looking man, very sure of himself and his position in life. She couldn't tell how this could be as without her father he would probably be reduced to nothing again, but she could feel the power and assurance almost flowing out of him. She could also sense a lot of things she was unable to put a name to, and it was these unknown factors which instinctively frightened her.

She wanted to explain about helping Raissa Sibour with her three children, but she was suddenly unable to. If Stein believed the worst of her, didn't she deserve it? Soft words and sympathy would never make her feel she was atoning for what she had done. She felt like a prisoner, knowing she would never feel any better until she had suffered a hundred lashes, or at least its equivalent in some kind of punishment!

CHAPTER TWO

STEIN came closer to where she was standing and she could feel his sheer magnetism reaching out to her. His hands closed over her shoulders with a strength she found impossible to defy as he studied the fine bone structure of her face.

'You were always beautiful, Helen,' he murmured huskily. 'I can see how you would have enjoyed yourself in Paris.'

'I haven't been enjoying myself anywhere!' Helen allowed herself to protest this much. 'At least . . .' her voice faltered, 'not in the way I'm sure you mean.'

'Really?'

His glance continued its slow appraisal, and she squirmed. Was there to be no end to his mocking speculation? Her figure was good, but suddenly she hated the way his eyes were going cynically over it. She had a slender, supple body which men often stared at longer than her face, but she didn't usually appreciate such attention. Not when it managed to convey only sexual interest.

One of his hands left her shoulder to touch her smooth cheek. 'You have beautiful skin, like silk— flawless.'

Helen's blue eyes fixed helplessly on his as she tried not to shrink from him. Before, when she had known him, he had been kind. On the face of it, he still was, but somewhere there was a difference. As his head bent towards her, his purpose explicit, she withdrew with a faint gasp. 'Stein, please!'

Immediately he let go of her. 'It's scarcely the time, is it,' he said, with a flinty, derisory smile, 'with Lester barely cold in his grave?'

'No.' She bit her lip, realising he was as capable of cruelty as of kindness. Only if she could keep one step ahead of him might she be safe.

'Come,' he said suavely, as her thick lashes flickered and a faint colour stole into her face, 'I'll take you back to your room. If I were you I should try and get some rest before dinner.'

It was almost seven and Helen stood before the long mirror in her bedroom abstractedly studying her own reflection. Her dress looked distinctly shabby. Madame Sibour had insisted they changed for dinner and she had worn the dresses she had taken to France continually. Helen frowned. She might have to ask Stein if it would be possible to get an advance on the money she would inherit from her father. It wasn't something that had occurred to her until now that she definitely needed some new clothes.

She must have appeared more anxious than she realised, for in the dining-room Stein glanced at her keenly and asked quietly, 'More problems?'

'I shouldn't have,' she sighed, responding to the note of encouragement in his voice.

'What do you mean by that?' His brows met as she bent without appetite over her soup.

She had been aware of his eyes on her all the time they had been having a drink in the lounge. She wasn't to know he had been dwelling with resigned awareness on her sheer loveliness, which a year in France had done nothing to diminish. Helen had thought he was silently condemning her shabbiness and prodded herself into grasping the opportunity this seemed to offer.

'It's just my clothes,' she began hesitantly, lifting her head. 'Everything I have seems so terribly shabby and I was wondering if I could get some money to buy new ones. I would only need enough to tide me over until I see Mr Dent. Even though he's away, surely it must be possible for me to have a few pounds from Dad's estate?'

Stein said cynically, 'I didn't expect you to mention money this evening, but I might have known.'

'I shouldn't have done,' Helen's eyes clouded with hurt, 'but it was the way you were looking at me. I thought you were criticising my dress.'

'I wasn't looking at your dress,' he told her dryly.

'Apart from myself,' she added hurriedly, 'won't I need money to pay the staff?'

'There's no need to panic, though,' he observed coolly. 'I'll see to everything necessary.'

Helen was stung to retort. 'I have to begin managing my own affairs some time! If I borrowed money from you I'd only have to pay it back.'

'Oh, I'll make sure you do,' he assured her. 'Don't let that worry you.'

His gaze lingered on her so insolently she could almost feel her flesh beginning to heat. Unhappily she wished she had never mentioned her depleted finances, but she had hoped he would understand. Now she didn't know what to think. Getting through to Stein was like threading one's way through a minefield. She was never quite sure whether she was going to make it, or whether he was going to blow up.

'Didn't you have enough money in France?' she heard him enquire.

Again she had an urge to explain what she had been doing in France and what had happened to the cash her father had sent there. That Stein knew about it was obvious and she could tell by the glint in his eye that he was just waiting for her to deny receiving it. She wouldn't lie to him, nor would she seek to justify herself by telling the truth, although she knew that by keeping silent she might suffer the full weight of his wrath.

But this was the only way, she told herself feverishly. Only by suffering could she hope to get rid of her feelings of guilt. This had to happen before she could even begin to feel better. One didn't need to be brilliant to be able to think this out for oneself!

'I only had enough to get me home,' she said quickly, as Stein repeated his question.

'Did you have to keep your boy-friend as well?' he taunted, his eyes raking her mercilessly.

'No,' she muttered miserably. She ought to have said yes but she craved Stein's approval so desperately that she couldn't bear to condemn herself entirely. If she did, he might leave her and she couldn't somehow contemplate never seeing him again. Slightly dazed by her own inner vehemence, which she didn't quite understand, she found her eyes sliding away from him, this in itself seeming to contradict her feeble word of denial.

'God!' he muttered softly. 'How do you still manage to look so innocent?'

'Perhaps because I am,' she replied, her voice trembling.

'Remind me to prove you wrong some time,' he laughed without a hint of humour.

While they drank coffee Helen still smarted from the hurt of his derision. She felt no clearer about a lot of things but was determined to make an extra effort. Whatever the cost, she must let Stein go. She couldn't continue clinging to him like a vine, feeding on the sense of duty he obviously felt because she was his late partner's daughter.

'Stein,' she began, turning towards him, 'you don't have to stay here. I'm certain I can manage on my own. When Harold Dent arrives I'll have plenty of money and he'll tell me exactly how I stand. I promise I won't do anything drastic about the firm without consulting you.'

'I like living here,' he said absently, leaning against the mantelshelf of the fireplace in the library, to which they had sojourned after dinner as it was cosier than the lounge.

Helen sighed, wishing he would give her a straight answer. 'I won't need a housekeeper and two maids,' she went on stubbornly, 'but they can stay until they find other jobs.'

'You can forget about all that!' he said decisively, his dark face unmoving, as determined as her own.

He made Helen shiver as his eyes caught hers and wouldn't let her go. She felt so shaken that she was glad she was sitting in a chair and not standing beside him. A protest rose to her lips, but before she could voice it the telephone rang and Stein picked it up.

'Maddison,' he said abruptly. Then, 'Oh, hello, Barbara.' He listened, apparently uncaring that Helen was listening too—or trying to! 'Yes, tomorrow evening,' she heard him say, 'as we arranged.'

Who was Barbara? Helen wondered hollowly. When she had known Stein before she couldn't remember him going out with other women. He had been diligent in his pursuit of her and she had thought she was the only girl he was interested in. But that had been a year ago and there could be no disputing that he was extremely attractive to the opposite sex. He was no hermit either. Unhappily she recalled the rumours she had heard and blithely disregarded. Feeling slightly sick with regret, she tried not to stare at him. She was very sure no woman would be given the chance of rejecting him a second time!

After bringing his telephone call to a close, Stein returned to sit beside her on the couch. He reached for his coffee cup, then leant back to finish it, giving her a view of powerful muscles as he crossed his legs and the dark material of his trousers tightened. Hastily Helen averted her eyes, wondering why she should suddenly be conscious of such things, and why her heart should be racing madly when, on such a day, it ought to be too heavy almost to beat. She only wished for Stein's friendship, she told herself angrily. It was ridiculous to be reacting to him like an over-sexed schoolgirl!

'Your girl-friend?' She forced herself to glance at him and speak lightly.

'Jealous?' His brows rose sardonically as he took his cue from the indignant colour in her cheeks.

'No,' Helen denied, too quickly, 'of course not!'

'No?' He gave a slight smile, trailing his fingers down her wrist before taking her hand and raising her warm palm to his mocking lips. As she jerked it away, he said softly, 'When I kissed you yesterday you didn't find me so repulsive.'

This must be a chance to ask why he had kissed her, but a lack of confidence prevented her from grasping it. The moment passed and she murmured breathlessly, 'Yesterday was different.'

He laughed, gently taunting. 'Don't tell me you're suffering from a belated dose of conscience?'

'Obviously you aren't!' she retorted sharply.

Again his dark brows rose. 'Should I be? I'm not greatly troubled by my conscience.'

'You must owe my father a lot.'

'Ah, yes,' he murmured reflectively, 'so you once told me.'

Nervously Helen pleated her silky skirt. 'It may sound trite, but a little respect surely wouldn't come amiss?'

'You're probably quite right,' he said soberly.

'Anyway,' she rushed on, beset by a strange agitation, 'as you're seeing your girl-friend tomorrow, you won't have to restrain yourself much longer.'

'You have such a delicate way of putting things, Helen,' he grinned mockingly. 'You weren't always so tactful when it came to expressing yourself, especially over something which hurt you.'

Would he never forget her past behaviour? 'What you get up to doesn't hurt me,' she replied woodenly. 'And is it a crime to be young and impulsive? Perhaps while I've been away,' she admitted, 'I've learnt to stop and think before I speak.'

'I wonder?' Stein eyed her speculatively, his face

suddenly degrees colder. 'Perhaps you've learnt to be craftier, that's all.'

They were like strangers, at least Stein was looking at her as if she was one. To suspect he had some power over her seemed crazy. It was an indefinable feeling and like all such feelings was better ignored. So Helen reasoned as she remembered what she had just said and bit back an angry retort. She wouldn't convince Stein she had changed by shouting at him like a fishwife. She refused to ask herself why it was important that he should, even when her heart beat faster as she stared at him. When he rose with a sigh to pour himself a measure of brandy, she began talking quickly of other things.

Helen was up early next morning and after drinking the cup of tea one of the maids brought her, went for a walk in the grounds. Despite the size of the staff, there would be plenty for her to do in the house. For a start she would have to go through her father's things. But she would wait until Stein left for London before doing anything. He would probably be having breakfast and she had no wish to interrupt him. Perhaps tomorrow, if she could get hold of someone about some money, she might go to London with him and buy some new clothes.

Having imagined him having breakfast or already on his way to town, she was startled to see him striding towards her. He looked so fit and refreshed that she wondered if he had been out riding. After they had exchanged rather guarded greetings and she asked, he nodded.

'Yes,' he said, 'I enjoy it.'

Helen paused uncertainly beside him, a trim figure in her jeans and soft sweater, her fair, silky hair blowing like a mane behind her in the cold winter wind. He studied her coolly, with an interest she tried not to be aware of. Frost in the air had tinted her cheeks with enchanting colour, but it was something in Stein's grey eyes which made them feel suddenly burning.

'Do you ride a lot?' She swallowed, his close surveillance affecting her oddly.

'Quite a lot.' His eyes had darkened a little. 'You should try it.'

It wasn't something he had suggested before as he knew she was nervous of horses. 'No, thanks,' she declined lightly, and had no intention of allowing him to change her mind. 'Dad's horse will have to go, anyway,' she sighed, 'along with the house.'

'The house? What are you talking about?'

'It's much too big for one,' she said briefly. 'I've just been looking at it. It would be ridiculous to live here on my own.'

'Your grandfather's father built it, I believe?'

'Yes,' she shrugged as Stein turned towards it, 'but it's no use being sentimental.'

'You might get married,' he suggested, 'and have two or three kids. A lot of space could come in handy.'

'I haven't even met anyone yet!' she retorted. 'It would be foolish to keep a house this size waiting for something which might never happen.'

'You shouldn't have any problems.' Again his eyes inspected the early morning beauty of her face, the sensuous promise of her mouth and figure which the faint shadows under her eyes merely seemed to emphasise.

Helen flushed as his glance darkened and he came a step nearer. He was a strong man, powerful physically and mentally. He had always been able to make her quiver, and only when he kept his distance did she feel relatively safe.

'I think I'll concentrate on the house,' she said, 'rather than on a mythical husband and family.'

'Well, you can't do anything until you've seen your solicitor,' Stein said smoothly.

'I know,' she nodded impatiently.

'Have you seen the pool yet?' He raised a hand to

lift her jacket collar against the icy wind, a protective gesture which made her throat tighten, especially when his fingers caught her bare skin. 'It might just make you change your mind about selling.'

'The pool?' she exclaimed, suddenly tense. 'When was this put in? I had no idea . . .'

'Didn't your father tell you?' Stein sounded surprised.

'No, he did not,' Helen replied sharply.

'Perhaps that was because you never answered his letters,' Stein said, his wide mouth unsmiling. 'He used to say he could tell you a lot more, but he might only be wasting his time.'

Helen knew she deserved that and she couldn't blame Stein for pointing it out. 'I'm sorry,' she said humbly.

Silently he took her arm to guide her around the corner of the house along a path leading to one of the outbuildings. The contact brought her close to him and the strength amazingly seemed to leave her limbs as she stumbled and his grip tightened. She was so shaken by the fiery sensation that rushed through her that she was relieved beyond measure when he released her to open a door.

Once inside the building, she saw a large swimming pool with tiled surrounds, tastefully decorated. 'It must have cost the earth!' she gasped.

'Not exactly,' Stein cast a sardonic glance at her astonished face. 'Actually it was fairly easy to convert. The barn was already there. It was just a matter of digging a hole in the middle and laying a few pipes.'

'But I don't remember Dad ever swimming,' she muttered blankly.

'He didn't.'

'Don't tell me he had this done specially for guests? Or was it for you?' she asked incredulously.

'For you, actually.' Stein's eyes hardened. 'He thought if we had something like this you might be more inclined to stay at home.'

'A pool!' she breathed, frowning. 'But how . . .?'

'Oh, you know,' he rejoined coolly, 'parties by it, that kind of thing.'

'And you didn't encourage him?'

Stein said harshly, 'I didn't discourage him, once he had the idea firmly fixed in his head it would have been difficult.'

Helen averted her eyes from his hard, relentless face to gaze over the water.

'It's heated,' he said. 'You can use it any time.'

It was certainly tempting. Helen had swum a lot in France, where many households boasted a pool. If only she could be sure this hadn't been installed entirely on Stein's persuasion, and for his benefit, not hers. She hated to think Stein had been feathering his own nest. If her father hadn't died how much more might he have been persuaded to spend? As always, quick tears came to her eyes when she thought of her father, but she quickly blinked them away. She wanted desperately to be friends with Stein, but he was making it very difficult.

'Aren't you going to London today?' She pretended to lose interest in the pool. Suddenly she felt stifled as her thoughts threatened to suffocate her. She needed time to think.

'Not this morning,' his eyes narrowed slightly, 'maybe later.'

Why was he in no hurry? Hadn't her father so often crowed about Stein's dedication to duty, the amount of work he was capable of getting through in half the time of other men? As she glanced at him now, at the dark, brooding features stamped by more than a hint of ruthlessness, it wasn't difficult to believe. What she didn't understand was his willingness this morning to forget about business and remain by her side. He might have forgiven her, but the occasional glimpse of something she sometimes caught in his eyes made her doubt it.

As they left the barn which housed the pool, she

intended returning to the house. 'I haven't had breakfast yet,' she said, suspecting that he had.

'You won't starve for a few more minutes,' Stein smiled smoothly. 'Come and see the horses. There's a beautiful little filly which Lester was sure would persuade you to take up riding again.'

Indignation almost overwhelmed Helen as curiosity drove her to accompany Stein to the stables. Her father had only kept one horse, but Stein talked as if the stables were full of them. And they must have discussed her shortcomings pretty thoroughly, along with everything else!

Helen was startled to count half a dozen horses in the stables, all turning their heads as Stein and she approached. Stein was no stranger to them, she saw immediately, as they whinnied a welcome and nuzzled him with damp noses. Again she was amazed. Before she had gone to France, the stables had been falling down, her father had kept his one mount elsewhere. Since then they had obviously been rebuilt.

'It must have cost a fortune!' she gasped incredulously, exactly as she had done when she had seen the swimming pool.

'Very nearly,' Stein agreed, shooting out a hand to keep her clamped to his side as she thought of running. He didn't voice his suspicions but continued about the stables. 'I saw to having them repaired. No sense in having them falling about our ears.'

He had been busy! Such diligence—and personal involvement—could only prove one thing, that Stein had hoped she would never return. Her father might have hoped otherwise, but Stein must have been praying she would stay away! All this and his anger when he had met her yesterday was sufficient evidence. Even if she hadn't been looking for any she would have had to be blind not to have seen it!

'Very nice,' she said dully, her full mouth tightening, in a way which had his twisting sardonically. 'At least the horses appear to be enjoying themselves. They look well-bred,' she ran her eyes over them deliberately, 'they should fetch a good price.'

'You wouldn't think of selling them?' he muttered flatly, a faint flush on his cheeks which she immediately put down to guilt.

'Why on earth should I be thinking of keeping them?' she taunted. 'You know what I'm like with horses?'

'It's not that, is it?' he accused, leaning against an upright spar after throwing her arm away as if he couldn't bear to touch her any more. His eyes icy grey, he stared down at her. 'Already you're converting everything to money, thinking of all this only in terms of cash!'

'Why not?' she retorted, forgetting to control her anger, feeling incredibly reckless. If he thought money meant that much to her, well, let him!

He laughed, and it wasn't a pleasant sound. 'I imagine the men you lived with in France paid well for the privilege. How many men did you live with, by the way?' he asked insultingly.

'None.' She didn't expect he would believe her.

He didn't. 'You aren't even capable of telling the truth.'

Helen turned her back on him then. How could they be friends when he treated everything she said with contempt?

'Don't do that!' he jerked her around. 'Don't turn your back on me,' he rasped, 'I don't like it.'

She tried to push him away. 'And I don't like you touching me!'

'Once you didn't think you did, but you do now,' he threw the truth at her so devastatingly she had to deny it.

'You're crazy!' she cried furiously.

Stein drew her so close she could see the cold sparks in his eyes. 'Why must you always try and provoke me?' he muttered, his wrath suddenly matching her own as his lips descended to take hers in a long, cruel kiss.

Helen didn't know how long it lasted or when the pressure became almost more than she could bear. He ravished her mouth quite savagely, until she began feeling faint from the fires he lit in her body. The intenseness of raw passion burned through her veins while the tightening of his arms threatened to break her in two.

Yet strangely she found herself welcoming the molten sensation that fused them together as it hinted at exotic realms to be explored if once she was willing to surrender to the wildness of her emotions. As her arms went around his neck, she could no more have stopped them than she could have denied the discovery of her own deeply sensuous nature. She knew she should be fighting Stein, but instead she found she was having to fight the blind desire within herself to allow him complete domination. Was this frantic inclination to give in to him what she had been frightened of a year ago? she wondered dizzily. Was this what she had really fled from?

When he let her go she stared at him blindly, realising she might have found the answer to a query which had been puzzling her for months. At the same time another thought came to confuse her as she became aware she was still running. She couldn't tell Stein she cared for him, because she still didn't trust him—and she knew he knew it!

When he smiled slightly at her flushed, uneasy face and suggested casually, 'It might be a good idea if we got married,' doubt flashed in Helen's eyes as she suspected his reasons. A doubt which, from the wry twist of his mouth, he managed to interpret exactly.

Anger flared within her, swiftly removing all traces of the bewildering lethargy she had known in his arms. Whatever she felt, he had no right to joke about it. Of course from his point of view it would be convenient if she could be persuaded to marry him. She was, after all, the source of his income. And from her own angle, how many women would hesitate to take a man like Stein Maddison, regardless of his motives? Few, she suspected, but even if his proposal had been sincere, instead of an obvious feeler put out to see how she would receive it, she couldn't marry a man she didn't respect.

'I'm sure there must be an easier solution to your problems,' she retorted pointedly.

His voice held the hint of cruelty she was beginning to associate him with. 'The easy way never appealed to me. I wish it did.'

Helen fixed her eyes on the horses, who between tearing bits of hay continued regarding them curiously as they ate it. She remembered how she had avoided her father's attempts to teach her to ride for so long that in the end he had lost patience.

'A son of mine would have been riding like a veteran years ago!' he had accused the eight-year-old Helen.

Regardless of her choked protests, he had thrown her on the back of a flighty mare, and it wasn't until the horse had thrown her off again that he had given up. Not even he had been able to fight concussion and a badly broken arm. That was one thing about her father, she recalled with a bleak sigh, he had never been willing to alienate her completely. He had kept pushing her at obstacles a son might have taken in his stride, and when she failed he had usually lost his temper but drawn back. Whether affection had motivated his brief moments of remorse, or an acknowledgement of her less than masculine strength, Helen never did discover. He had never given her any obvious affection and she had never felt close enough to him to find the courage to ask if he loved her. According to Stein he had, and when she had gone away he had missed her.

'What else have you to show me?' she asked, suppressing a sigh as she turned to Stein with a shrug, meant to indicate that she wasn't impressed by his last statement.

'I'm not sure,' his smile deliberately taunted. 'I had tennis courts laid out in the old kitchen gardens at the back of the house. Do you play tennis, Helen?'

'Seldom in winter,' she replied, amazed. She wouldn't ask what more there was; already her digestion was having to work overtime! 'I suppose it all adds to the value of the property.'

'Naturally,' he clipped, a flare of irritation in his eyes at the apparent one-track direction of her mind. 'I wouldn't set your heart on selling, though. Not until you've seen Dent.'

Why did Stein keep telling her this? It bothered Helen all day. A terrible suspicion gripped her and she wondered why she hadn't thought of it before. Was it possible that her father had left the house to Stein? Could he do that? Surely the law protected a man's dependants from this kind of thing? But if Stein had persuaded her father to bequeath him the house, why had there been so much done to improve it? No, obviously her father, whatever his faults, had been thinking of her all the time. He had been too fond of money to spend it recklessly on anyone else.

Stein went off early to keep his date with the mysterious Barbara, who Helen had no doubt would also be beautiful. She flushed when she saw him dressed for the evening, realising, as she seemed too frequently to be doing, how good he looked. He told her he would probably stay in London for the night.

'In the flat?' she asked, feeling it suddenly necessary to know he didn't intend spending the whole night with Barbara.

'The flat?'

Was it fair that a man should have such expressive eyebrows? 'Dad's flat!' She tried not to be angry at what she believed to be his deliberate misunderstanding. She knew Stein used it occasionally. She couldn't recall that he'd ever had a place of his own. He must have done, of

course, before he had had the good fortune to bump
into her father, but it probably hadn't amounted to
much.

'Your father gave that up not long after you went
away,' Stein said coolly. 'I have my own—in the
Barbican. I think you would like it. It's very smart and
labour-saving. Everything happens at the push of a
button and the views over the City are superb.'

'And expensive!' Helen heard herself saying wasp-
ishly.

'Everything has to be paid for,' Stein nodded his
strong dark head. 'You must come and see for yourself
next time you're in town.'

She certainly would! Lowering her thick lashes to
hide her increasing suspicions, she grasped the
opportunity. 'I'll have to go for clothes. Could I come
with you?'

'Not this evening.'

'I didn't mean this evening!' Did he think she wanted
to play gooseberry! 'Just any time.'

'I shan't be back until late tomorrow. Business,' he
added sardonically, 'I'll ring you, if I get the chance.'

He touched her cheek, a careless gesture of farewell
while his eyes mocked. Yet when a flicker of electricity
shot though Helen from the brief contact, he removed
his hand as swiftly as she withdrew. He was paler but
otherwise controlled, and before she could speak
nodded curtly and left, leaving her shivering.

He might go out with other women, but somehow he
still found her rejection hard to take, Helen thought
with a hint of bitter satisfaction, thinking this had been
the reason for his abrupt departure.

He did ring next day to confirm that he wouldn't be
home in time for dinner. Helen was actually in bed
when he did arrive. She had gone early, hoping to avoid
him, and lay pondering on the changes she had found,
having grasped the opportunity his absence had offered
to thoroughly inspect the house and grounds. Obviously

a lot of money had been spent. Oakfield could now be classed as a show-place, and she had discovered two men employed to attend to the gardens alone, as well as a groom looking after the horses.

They had spoken to her respectfully and soberly, obviously remembering she had just suffered a bereavement, but they hadn't worn the anxious look of men who feared they were about to lose their jobs. Perhaps a new owner would keep them on. The more Helen saw, the more convinced she was there would have to be a new owner. Even if she retained her shares in the company she couldn't imagine receiving the kind of dividend which might be required to run Oakfield as it now was. Even the wages for the staff might be beyond her.

She had met the housekeeper, but Mrs Swinden wasn't the kind of woman she could talk to. Helen had to confess she didn't like her very much. She seldom took an instant dislike to anyone, but Mrs Swinden's manner had been little less than insolent. Helen wondered who had hired her. She would have to speak to Stein about her. It might not take long to sell the house, but even a small dose of Mrs Swinden might be too much! The sooner she was gone the better.

Helen's heart was heavy. If only one could put the clock back a few years! Her father might never have had much patience, but on the whole he hadn't been too difficult to live with. And, during the last few months she had been here, he had seemed to go out of his way to please her. Now she only had a horrible feeling of guilt which refused to go away, and on top of this everything seemed in such a dreadful muddle. She didn't even know where she stood with Stein and liked less how he could make her feel, especially when she couldn't be sure what his motives were.

The wind howled outside. It had blown all day, frosty and cold, and Helen hoped it wasn't going to snow. It blew around the chimneys, drowning every other sound, so when the door opened without warning she nearly jumped out of her skin. She stared at Stein, her eyes wide.

'What is it?' she whispered unsteadily. He was wearing a dark jacket and tie and looked extremely well groomed and fit. The energy and vitality in his face made her feel positively wilting, even though she was several years younger than he. He must have dined out again, although it wasn't late. The last time Helen had glanced at her watch it had only been eleven and he would have been an hour on the road.

He came in, closing the door, as if entering her room and enclosing them in such privacy wasn't unusual. With Helen's bewildered eyes on him he came and sat on the edge of her bed. He wasn't close, perhaps three feet away, but her heart began beating rapidly.

He returned her stare, his glance sliding to her throat where she suddenly realised her madly beating pulse must be betraying her.

When he didn't speak, she placed a nervous hand over it. 'You gave me a fright,' she said. 'You shouldn't have come here.'

'Why not?' he gazed at her steadily. 'Everyone's in bed.'

'I wasn't thinking of other people!' she gasped.

'Surely,' he mocked, 'you can't pretend you're frightened I might seduce you? I should imagine that happened with some other man, long ago?'

'If you've merely come to insult me——' she began angrily.

'I didn't think I was,' he interrupted tauntingly. 'A lot of girls would take it as a compliment, being judged attractive enough to arouse a man's desire. As for being able to satisfy it, of course, that's quite another matter.'

CHAPTER THREE

HELEN trembled, her cheeks hot with embarrassment and humiliation as Stein's contempt flicked her like a whiplash. He had never talked to her like this before. He might have teased her, when she had first known him, but always behind his raillery there had been a warm gentleness. Often she had thought he had been determined to protect her from the seamier side of life. Now he seemed all set to shock her.

She stared at him mutinously but decided to accept his insults without protest as part of the sackcloth and ashes course she felt she must tread because of her father.

'I'm sure you don't want me that way,' she answered flatly.

His eyes narrowed, moving slowly over her, his mouth twisting. 'How do you know how I want you?'

Silently she shook her head, unable to face his grim speculation. 'I'm tired, Stein,' she sighed.

'Exhausted from too much thinking, I would say,' he judged with an accuracy she hated. 'Perhaps you need a break, if only to do a little shopping.'

'Shopping?' She sat up, clutching the sheet which fell from her satin-strapped but otherwise bare shoulders. Some of the despondency faded from her eyes as she exclaimed eagerly, 'You'll take me to London?'

'If you really need clothes.'

'I do!' She had to make him believe it. She didn't want him to think she would bother with anything so trivial, at a time like this, unless it was necessary. 'I didn't take much to France, only enough to fill one suitcase, but I can't find any of the things I left behind. They seem to have disappeared.'

'I think your father threw most of them out,' Stein shrugged. 'Someone came collecting for a jumble sale and he thought it was better that some charity had them, rather than the moths.'

'He certainly made a good job of it,' she muttered, with a little indignation.

'He wanted your room decorated, for when you came back,' Stein recalled. 'He decided it would be easier if the wardrobes were empty, but he didn't see to it personally, he asked me to do it for him.'

Helen flushed at the thought of Stein's hands on her most intimate possessions. She had bought quite a lot during the last few months before she had gone to France. Crazy scraps of satin and lace which she had worn under the skimpy dresses in which she had gone to her parties. It had been part of the subconscious defiance which had driven her continually to try and shock Stein. He had been more bored than shocked, she suspected, lowering his heavy lashes so he wouldn't see her unhappy agitation.

Making an effort to change the subject, she queried, 'He had the whole house redecorated?'

'It was necessary,' Stein said shortly. 'We began doing a lot of entertaining. Foreign visitors like our old English mansions, as long as they're not too shabby.'

'How did you manage without a hostess?' Helen frowned. Her father had never been keen on having friends in, although he had frequently dined out. This new innovation must have been Stein's idea. She wondered who had footed the bills.

'We usually found someone willing to oblige,' she heard Stein saying.

'Such as Barbara?'

'She did on one or two occasions,' he admitted with a smile.

Suddenly Helen didn't want to talk about Barbara or any of the other women Stein knew and made use of. 'If

I sell Oakfield,' she said sharply, 'you'll have to entertain in your flat.'

'Sometimes I do,' he replied, his eyes glinting.

'About tomorrow,' Helen said quickly, as she imagined the kind of entertainment that would be and her gibe appeared to leave him unmoved, 'what time will you be leaving?'

'About ten,' he viewed her pink cheeks idly. 'We don't have to hurry.'

She was disapprovingly silent for a moment. 'What about the firm? Surely you have more to do since—since . . .'

'Helen!' he cut through her halting speech effectively, 'I wish you'd stop worrying! Nothing I say seems to make any difference, but the firm isn't taking any harm, I assure you.'

'If you say so.' She raised wide, anxious eyes to his face.

He stood up but to her dismay sat down again, this time much closer. Beneath his jacket his shoulders were wide and powerful, filling her vision so that she couldn't see anything but him. Trembling slightly, she wondered if she could ask him to sit elsewhere.

'Tomorrow,' he said, looking about as open to suggestion as a leopard on the prowl, 'I'm devoting to you.'

'You don't have to come shopping with me, though!'

'Did you think I was going to let you roam around London on your own?' he asked impatiently. 'You're headstrong and reckless and highly-strung. You haven't had time to get over your father yet. What would happen if you fainted or were taken ill suddenly and I wasn't there?'

It was unlikely, Helen thought, but she couldn't resist what she was too willing to construe as concern. If Stein was worried he must care for her a little. Unless—doubts rushed back—unless he intended making sure she didn't meet another man? Someone she might impulsively develop a raging passion for, which would really upset his applecart!

Helen swallowed. Could she afford to argue? There was a warning glint in his eyes and he had only to touch her for her whole body to burn. His temper was unpredictable. If she argued and he shook her she didn't know how she might react. Between them there was some kind of fairly explosive chemistry and neither admitting nor hiding it would make it go away. Close at hand, the sheer sexual force of Stein was something she was all too aware of, and while she hated her own body for its blind response, she was finding it increasingly difficult to resist. She could only pray that given time she would learn how to cope with it.

Their eyes met and the darkness of his had a curious effect on her. Her nerves began jumping violently while a fierce warmth began invading her body. She had to get rid of him, if she wasn't to make a fool of herself!

Nervously she managed to smile. 'I'll be ready at ten.'

As if conscious of her nervousness and scornful of it, Stein swooped to drag her swiftly to him. When she tried to struggle, he muttered contemptuously against her trembling mouth, 'Be still—I'm only taking a goodnight kiss, as you so obviously want rid of me.'

If that were all! Helen's senses screamed, as she tried to control that part of her outside her intelligence. How was it that her mind so quickly lost the battle when Stein attacked her physically? For the first time in her life she was experiencing male domination to which her body clamoured to surrender. Maybe Stein had always been a threat, but when he exerted pressure she found it shattering.

His hands were in her hair, his painful grip preventing any movement, throwing her completely at his mercy, while the bruising insistence of his mouth forced her submission. And it wasn't until he felt her response that he set her free. Only then did he thrust her from him, his eyes gleaming with a cool satisfaction when her arms lifted to creep around him.

'Sleep well, Helen,' he smiled cynically, 'I'll see you in the morning.'

She was up early, as she scarcely slept at all. When she did it was only fitful dozing split by vivid dreams from which she awoke exhausted. By the time a winter's dawn reluctantly entered her room she was pale-faced and heavy-eyed, her body still restless with a dissatisfaction she didn't understand. Some time in the early morning she had given up trying to measure the extent of Stein's hold over her. Her heart ached, whenever she thought of him, in a way she didn't like. She suspected, if she allowed it, that she might soon be in love with him, and this she was desperate to avoid. It had to be easier when the house was sold and their meetings thereafter limited strictly to business, if at all. Pray God this happened very soon! Helen breathed feverishly as she half fell out of bed and stumbled to the bathroom to take a reviving cold shower.

Stein didn't join her until it was time to leave, but she could tell from his air of vital freshness that he hadn't just got up. Obviously he had been out, riding her horses and sampling her pool! She greeted him distantly, her eyes cool.

'Tried the pool yet?' he asked, when they were on their way.

'Er—what was that?' Helen blinked at him, not having heard a word he said. She had been too busy studying the back of the chauffeur's head as they purred smoothly towards London. This morning the car was a Mercedes, and she had a sudden desire to ask if it was one of a fleet, and who owned them.

She dared not ask, much as she would have liked to. She guessed from the sharp amusement in Stein's eyes that he knew what she was thinking, and was waiting. Biting her lip hard, she prayed that her never-ending suspicions would leave her. The struggle with them against her desire to trust Stein was wearing her down.

She realised she was making mental lists all the time of things which might prove his dishonesty, and she didn't know whether to be disgusted with herself or whether to encourage such shrewish instincts as sensible.

'The pool?' Stein repeated, with the odd, deliberate impatience Helen was no nearer understanding but which she was becoming used to, 'I imagined you in it, all day.'

'I had no time,' she replied hastily, flushing as his gaze seemed to insolently strip her, in a way that brought heat to her body as well as her cheeks.

His eyes narrowed. 'Why not?' he asked coolly.

'I don't know,' she muttered evasively. 'You forget I haven't been home for a year. I just wanted to look around.'

His smile was taunting rather than sympathetic. 'I find your sentiments difficult to believe in when all you can think of is getting rid of the place.'

'Selling something isn't always the same as getting rid of it,' she retorted stiffly, adding, as he looked—or pretended to look—bewildered, 'Sometimes it's necessary!'

'Be sure you know what is,' he remarked ironically.

'I didn't know we had a chauffeur!' she snapped.

Stein ignored this. 'You think the best way to ward off an attack is to get in first?' He relaxed with a slight grin. 'Hasn't anyone ever told you there are smarter ways?'

'I don't know what you're talking about!' she said sullenly, hating his intelligent astuteness almost as much as the things he indirectly accused her of.

When his brows rose slightly, as she had known they would, her eyes slipped lower on his face. She didn't realise how intent her glance was as she closely examined his hard-hewn features. Each time she looked at him she felt she had never seen him before, and a sudden sense of panic, as she stared at his mouth, made her breathing shallow, so that her breast rose and fell quickly. She was knocked completely off balance and her nails were piercing her palms before she recovered herself again.

Stein was wearing a dark suit. It moulded his powerful body flatteringly but was, nevertheless, formal. Helen thought he might have changed his mind about coming with her.

'Are you going to the office?' she asked, feeling she might breathe easier if she kept her mind on other things apart from his face.

'No,' he replied abruptly, 'I told you.'

'Yes.' She couldn't argue with such implacable tones, such a relentless expression. 'I just wondered . . .'

'That's your trouble,' he snapped. 'You wonder far too much, as I keep telling you.'

Helen was relieved when they reached London, with the tension between them so thick she thought it could have been cut with a knife. If contained a kind of violence that made her shiver. Whenever she looked out of the window she could feel Stein's glance sliding to her, the impression of dislike so realistic she had to use every bit of willpower she possessed to stop herself from flinching.

The chauffeur, whom Stein called Paul, dropped them off outside a famous department store. Helen couldn't hear what instructions Stein gave the man before he drove away.

'What time did you arrange for him to pick us up?' she frowned after him as he disappeared in the fast stream of traffic.

'You don't have to look as if your one lifeline has deserted you,' Stein mocked. 'At a guess you'll be safer with me than Paul. I'm surprised we didn't crash several times this morning. He spent more time looking at you through his mirror than at the road.'

'Don't be silly,' she retorted coldly, tossing back her fair head.

Stein seemed more interested in the line of her throat and how the winter sunshine caught the burnished masses of her hair. 'You must have noticed the way men look at you,' he said, somewhat dryly. 'At the funeral I thought it positively indecent.'

She flushed. 'Why don't you come right out and tell me I encourage it?' she challenged sharply. 'I don't remember receiving that kind of attention. There were a lot of strangers there. I expect they were just curious.'

Stein cast her a speculative glance as they made their way through the store. 'A lot of those strangers,' he emphasised the word, 'were old business colleagues of your father's. How come you didn't know them?'

Helen bit her lip indecisively. She had been away at school and during the holidays she had never seen much of her father. He had seldom entertained or introduced her to any of his associates, not even after she had joined the firm. Once, when she had asked him the very same question Stein was asking her now, he had said he didn't believe in mixing business with pleasure. If Stein had managed to alter his views on the subject it was more than she had ever been able to do!

A fleeting resentment because of this caused her to shrug instead of attempting to explain. 'I was away a lot,' she hedged.

Stein took it the way she had known he would. 'Painting the town red, I suppose?'

She saw his broad shoulders lift the merest fraction and his face harden again, and irrationally her heart sank as she realised how willing he was to believe the worst of her. If she suffered no other retribution for her recent neglect of her father, Stein's condemnation might be enough!

Because of a fresh wave of depression which almost overwhelmed her, Helen lost no time in choosing new clothes. She bought recklessly without bothering to look at price tags. Her father had never been very generous with pocket money, not until she'd left the office anyway. Then, as if to try and compensate for taking away her job, he had given her more than he had ever allowed her before, but she hadn't had time to acquire the habit of spending really freely.

This morning she didn't pause to think how much this shopping spree was costing. Swiftly she accumulated what she thought she might need over the next few months. It would save time, later, if she didn't have to keep running in and out of shops. There would be an enormous amount to do if she had to sell the house and look for a new job.

While she was making her mind up about various items Stein lounged in a chair and watched her, but to her relief he never offered an opinion. When she disappeared in a cubicle to try on a dress, he didn't ask to see her in it or try to persuade her to alter a decision. His eyes followed her everywhere, much, she suspected, to the model-like salesgirl's chagrin, but throughout the whole procedure, he maintained a grim, tight-lipped silence.

'Why don't you try smiling for a change?' Helen hissed, feeling curiously on edge because of his unremitting attention. 'If you don't, she——' with a meaningful glance at the momentarily diverted assistant, 'will begin to suspect you're a typical penny-pinching husband!'

'When I'm your husband people will know, it's not something they'll speculate about,' he rejoined harshly.

Helen drew back as though stung, wishing she had never said anything. It had been a crazy thing to come out with. With Stein it seemed she could never act normally, but did she have to let him know? He was joking, of course, about being her husband, but it must be her fault for suggesting it in the first place.

'I'm sorry, Stein.' Her wide blue eyes appealed to him unhappily from her hot face.

'So you should be,' he retorted softly, his grey eyes coolly unforgiving.

Helen asked Stein if the account could be sent to her and she could settle as soon as she had seen Harold

Dent. He shook his head and replied that it would be easier to have everything put on his account. Helen didn't feel too happy about this, but before she could protest he was making the necessary arrangements. He asked for her new clothes to be packed so that his chauffeur could pick them up later. His air of authority was unmistakable. Why, Helen wondered bitterly, did no one ever question it?

'Was this where you got the outfit I'm wearing?' she asked as they left the store for lunch. She wasn't fond of black, although she knew the colour suited her and was the only suitable thing she had had for London. She had almost worn her jeans, she was sure her father wouldn't have minded, but because of Stein her courage had failed her.

'No, I didn't get it here.' He took her arm to halt her on the busy pavement.

She tried not to think of the exclusive label. Another bill he would no doubt, in due course, present her with! 'You did a good job,' she said lightly. 'Everything fits.'

'I remembered your size,' he shrugged briefly, as they stepped inside a taxi.

It was quite late before they finished eating at a famous hotel, not renowned for its cheap prices. Helen, surprised to discover she was hungry, wished dismally that she could stop thinking of the cost when Stein encouraged her to try the most expensive dishes. It was futile warning herself he might guess what she was thinking. He seemed able to read her thoughts no matter how hard she tried to conceal them.

Earlier she had toyed with the idea of calling on her father's solicitor, but she didn't get the opportunity, because Stein never left her. She sighed and gave up. Stein had asked her not to and she might be wiser to obey him. In only a few more days Harold Dent would be coming to see her at Oakfield.

Around four, Stein said he must visit his flat as he had some papers to pick up among other things. Helen hoped he might leave her, but he insisted that she came along. She didn't refuse as again she was filled with a suspicious curiosity she found impossible to resist.

She missed the ironic twist of Stein's lips as he waved down another taxi.

'You'll like it,' he told her as they were borne swiftly towards the City.

Helen had become used to having wine with her meals in France, but she had usually limited herself to one glass. Today, during lunch, she had imbibed much more than she normally did in an effort to rid herself of the obsession she appeared to be developing regarding Stein and her money. If he was trying, or was going to try and do her out of it, she would know soon enough! If he had contrived to cheat her father, she would learn about that too. Somehow she couldn't believe Stein was guilty of any of these things, even while the evidence was definitely against him.

She saw it now, despite the wine which hazed her mind as they entered the luxurious apartment in the magnificent Barbican complex. It was superb! There was no other word for it. Helen drew a sharp breath, trying to conceal her stunned surprise. It had everything!

'Like it?' Stein asked carelessly, watching her expressive face.

'Who wouldn't?' she tried to match his mood. 'It must be a nice place to live—if you can afford it.'

'The area isn't cheap.' He threw off his jacket with a sigh of relief.

She swallowed, noticing the strength of his shoulders straining against his thin shirt. Through it she could see the dark tangle of hair on his chest and she wished he had kept his coat on.

'Make yourself at home.' His eyes ran restlessly over her slim figure. 'I want to sort out those papers I mentioned as well as making a few phone calls. There's a kitchen which I seldom use, but you might find enough to make us a cup of tea or coffee, while I'm busy.'

When he had gone, Helen removed her own coat and wandered into the kitchen. It didn't look like a kitchen; it looked like something out of one of those space ships one sometimes saw on television! The steel and chrome were dazzling, the tiles on the floor so spotless she doubted if they had ever known a human foot. She supposed as it was a service flat Stein just rang for meals when he wanted them and this saved him the bother of employing a housekeeper.

Before the kettle boiled the doorbell rang, its melodious chimes echoing round her. It rang again, and as Stein didn't appear to answer it, she decided she had better go herself.

A beautiful, dark-haired girl stood outside and gazed at Helen enquiringly as she opened the door. 'I haven't seen you before,' she said coolly. 'What on earth are you doing here?'

Helen's eyes widened at the girl's tone. She clearly wasn't accustomed to seeing other girls in Stein's flat, but Helen didn't appreciate her icy stare.

'Just looking,' she returned, tongue in cheek but quite truthfully, for that was almost all she had done so far.

The other girl frowned, but while she was obviously trying to decide whether Helen was just naturally dimwitted or trying to make a fool of her, Stein appeared.

'Oh, Stein!' The girl pushed past Helen with an exaggerated sigh of relief. 'I rang Oakfield, but they told me you were in town and your secretary said you might be here.'

'Barbara!'

Helen stood flattened against the door watching them. So this was the mysterious Barbara? She slid her arm through Stein's and hung on tightly, murmuring that she had missed him and wouldn't mind a drink. As Stein glanced down on her, a faint smile on his face, something stirred inside Helen, a pain that made her flinch.

'If you'll excuse me, I think I hear the kettle boiling,' she said.

As if her voice made the other two suddenly remember she was there, they both turned their heads and looked at her.

'Have you been engaging a maid, darling?' Barbara asked coldly.

Helen could have slapped the mocking quirk from Stein's mouth as he studied the white tea-towel draped round her waist. Over her black dress it might just have passed for a uniform.

'I'm considering her.'

'I'd send her packing,' to Helen's astonishment Barbara apparently took him seriously. 'She's far too young, for one thing. I know we would all like to help the unemployed, but I'm renowned for my incredible intuition. She'd be nothing but trouble, darling.'

'My sentiments exactly,' he agreed solemnly.

'Don't you think the joke's gone far enough?' Helen snapped. If Stein felt like having fun he wasn't having it at her expense!

'You aren't a maid?' If anything the frown on Barbara's face deepened and her voice spiralled.

'I'm sorry to disappoint you,' Helen wasn't slow to detect the anger in the other girl's voice but made no attempt to hide her own irritation, 'but I'm afraid you can't get rid of me by asking Stein to give me the sack. Now, if you'll excuse me——'

She banged the kitchen door on Barbara's voluble indignation and Stein's soothing murmurs. The room was full of steam and she hastily switched off the kettle. Taking a teapot from a cupboard, she thumped it down on a gleaming surface, but it didn't make her feel any better. If Barbara was a bitch, so was she, she reminded herself forcibly. Barbara might not have anything to be humble about, but she had! She'd be willing to bet

Barbara was no innocent little virgin, as she was, but that shouldn't make her feel superior. Not when the sins of Helen Davis far outweighed her virtues! Beneath her temper, Barbara might be frank and honest—well, she was certainly frank! But if Barbara had been in her shoes she might never have treated her father and his partner so badly!

Full of remorse, Helen made tea and put three cups on a tray. Making a great effort to look pleasant, she picked the tray up and returned to the hall. It was empty. She went to the lounge. It was empty too. Where was everyone?

'Looking for somebody?'

Stein had the kind of voice generally able to charm birds off trees. Helen did her best to ignore the way it teased her nerves.

'Yes, I am!' she flushed as she remembered how she had vowed to eat humble pie. 'I'm sorry, Stein. I made some tea. I was looking for you.'

'Three cups?' he said, counting.

'There are three of us . . .'

'There were,' he smiled grimly, 'until you put your foot in it!'

'I didn't think she'd be so easily defeated!' Helen grinned.

Stein's eyes became glacial. 'I wasn't aware you were fighting a battle, Helen, but I warn you, don't insult any friends of mine.'

Helen's flush returned as she repeated. 'I'm sorry, Stein, I didn't mean to upset her. I'll apologise when I see her again.'

'If you see her again!'

Helen glanced at him quickly. Did he intend keeping them apart, or was he finished with Barbara? She lowered her thick lashes slightly, surprised to find she still had enough courage to put out a feeler. 'Miss—er——?' she halted enquiringly.

'Bates,' Stein supplied coolly.

'—seems very nice.'

'She can be.' As Helen, suddenly realising she was still holding the tray put it down on a low table, he stared at her narrowly.

'What did she want?' Helen ventured, judging him to be more approachable. She should have sat down, but she felt too restless.

He smiled slightly, a smile that made Helen feel startlingly angry.

'You, I suppose?' she spoke involuntarily.

'Do you find it surprising?' he countered dryly.

'No,' she confessed, but refused to look at him. It was enough that he must hear the sigh in her voice. She didn't want him to see what might lie in her eyes.

'Ah, a little honesty at last!' He crossed to where she was standing and lifted her hot face to his, his gaze wandering closely over the beauty of her features, coming to rest on her tender, exquisitely shaped mouth. 'It makes a nice change, if you mean it.'

'It needn't be personal,' she said tersely.

'So you can take me or leave me?' he taunted. 'Like something which catches your attention in a shop window and the next moment is forgotten.'

If only she could! Carefully she tried to edge from him, reluctant to struggle. The way he held her head made the hair spill over her shoulders, like skeins of blonde silk, as the angle of her slender, willowy body bent backwards. His fingers tightened and held. They began burning her skin, slowly dissolving her desire for escape. She trembled, wondering how it happened, her mind slowly recognising its master. They might have been fused completely, as one. It was crazy, but she could actually feel the heat flowing out of him, penetrating every corner of her being.

'It's ridiculous!' she gasped, determined to deny such incredible sensations.

Stein presumed she was commenting on his last observation. 'Our conversation, you mean? Maybe I agree. Talking never gets us anywhere. This remains our best line of communication, although I don't expect you ever to admit it.'

Unable to move, she stared at him as he mockingly lowered his head. He took his time, as if he knew she was incapable of resisting. In a kind of trance she watched him coming nearer, her eyes dilating as he slowly found her mouth.

His lips were firm and warm, her heavy lashes fell as she succumbed to their gentle pressure. Then, as passion leapt between them, the transitory moment passed and she found herself clinging to him. They merged, like a storm on a dark winter's night, as Stein continued to kiss her and once more her senses were flung into turmoil.

The doorbell rang again.

'That must be Paul,' Stein sighed against her lips, feeling them quiver. 'Are you ready to go home?'

Helen couldn't answer, not immediately. It was all she could do to open her eyes. There was no tenderness in Stein's face, none of the frantic emotion she was experiencing. His eyes were darker, but filled only with a certain irony.

Numbly she nodded to the question in his glittering, downbent gaze as he released her.

'I shan't be more than ten minutes,' he said. 'Paul can wait.'

She tried to shake herself out of an overwhelming daze, envying Stein his hard composure. Bitterness at such unshakeable assurance rose. In another man it might have seemed exaggerated, but not with him, damn him! She hated the arrogant tilt to his dark head that seemed to intensify the brilliance of the grey eyes coolly resting on her. What wouldn't she have given to have seen him trembling just once, as she was doing!

'Let Paul in and give him a cuppa in the kitchen,' he muttered briefly, 'but that's all.'

Helen frowned, her eyes widening in disbelief.

'Don't say it,' he snapped. 'I do mean what you think I mean!'

The urge to hit him grew stronger, only restrained by a strange kind of sickness. 'I'll wait in here,' she replied dully, 'after I've made him his tea.'

'Good.' Stein suddenly relented. 'Once I'm through, I'll give you a quick tour of the place, if you like——'

Helen's spirit hadn't been totally extinguished. 'Now that is something to look forward to!' she cried swiftly, turning her back on him with a truly feminine flounce.

Angry fingers closed around her wrist, pulling her back to him, stirring her blood and making her pulses quicken.

'I told you, don't do that!'

'How else do I leave you?' Her blue gaze challenged him heatedly. 'Do I back away from you with little bows? Is that what you'd like?'

'You know what I'm getting at.' He wasn't taking her seriously, but there was a warning glint in his eyes, 'Have your fun, if you must, but be sure you don't live to regret it.'

'I wonder you have the nerve to threaten me, Mr Maddison!' Helen exclaimed, his hold over her both physically and mentally driving her a little too near total madness. 'I do own a lot you'd like to get your hands on. Maybe even half this flat?'

His lids lowered, as swiftly as hers often did, but she was beyond noticing. Later she was to realise she had missed a lot of obvious clues.

'That being the case,' he drawled, 'you might be asked to donate towards a new doorbell, seeing that Paul appears determined to wear the present one out.'

Oh, Stein was shameless! She had to admire such total lack of conscience! He had all but admitted what she had suspected all along. Had he hoped she wouldn't realise? Had all those ruthless, unavoidable—she used the word with emphasis to drown any suggestion of her own responsiveness—kisses been used as part of a programme to bring her to her knees? It could be the answer, for his hatred on their way from the airport had been too real to be disguised, even if he had tried hard to hide it since.

No, he was merely playing a game with her, attempting to pull the wool over her eyes, while his sultry mistress—the worst villains always had them— waited impatiently in the background! Stein probably hadn't intended she should meet Barbara, which must explain why he had got rid of her so quickly. No one, unless they had something to hide, would normally have disposed of anyone so ruthlessly.

The painful implications of this shook Helen with something more devastating than anger as Stein let go of her sardonically and she went to let Paul in.

CHAPTER FOUR

WHEN the kettle boiled Helen made a fresh pot of tea and decided to share it with Paul. What did it matter what Stein thought? He might be annoyed if he found out, but she couldn't go much lower in his estimation.

'I'm not annoying you, am I?' Paul asked.

'No, of course not,' she flushed, quickly smoothing the frown from her face. 'I was thinking of something else.'

Paul nodded, relaxing, stirring three spoonfuls of sugar in his tea.

She watched, fascinated. 'Is all that sugar good for you, do you think?'

'If I drank much tea it mightn't be.'

He had a gentle, cultured voice, contrasting oddly with his rather bold eyes. 'Have you worked for Mr Maddison long?' she asked.

'Almost a year,' he replied briefly, 'since I left university.'

'You couldn't find anything else?'

'I'm looking all the time,' he grinned, 'but jobs aren't easy to find.'

'No,' she sighed, considering her own, untrained chances.

'I'd rather do anything than sit around,' Paul shrugged. 'I don't suppose I'd be driving for Mr Maddison if my father hadn't known him.'

'Really?' Interest kindled in Helen's eyes, but Stein had to choose that moment to stalk into the kitchen.

'I'll show you around now, Helen, if you're ready.'

His fingers curved on her arm, this and his tone suggesting a degree of possessiveness she didn't like. It took all her control to smile at him instead of shaking him off. 'I'm ready,' she said, putting down her teacup.

In one of the bedrooms he drawled, 'Don't look at me so suspiciously. I don't intend kissing you again, not with young Paul waiting.'

Her eyes widened as she stared at him frostily. The effect might have been better, she realised, if her cheeks hadn't been so pink. 'Paul's been to university,' she retorted. 'Couldn't you find him something better to do?'

'Depends what you mean by better,' he said.

'You know what I mean!'

'I'm trying,' Stein replied mildly, 'but it's difficult. All the same, he's a very bright young man. Don't encourage him.'

'Should that make sense?'

'If you think about it.'

Helen gazed rather blindly around the very masculine apartment, mostly decorated in black and white. Did Stein suspect every man was after her because of her money? People often suspected others of the same vices they harboured themselves!

'This is rather stark, isn't it?' She had to make some comment to hide her anger.

'I've never noticed.'

'Some people like it this way.' Her roving glance concentrated suddenly. Plain and simple it might be, but obviously expensive!

'Yes,' Stein agreed absently, his glance wandering from her to the bed.

Helen wondered how he could raise her pulse rate so easily—and the impulsive side of her temper. 'You didn't make it clear before when I asked,' she exclaimed. 'Does half of this belong to the firm? That is me?' she added tightly.

'No, this is mine own,' he quoted dryly.

'But no ill-favoured thing!' she commented in similar tones.

'You don't believe me?'

She backed from something she was sure was menace in his voice. 'I didn't say that!'

'Don't insult me by implying that I'm a fool as well as a thief!' he grated, his eyes suddenly as angry as hers had been.

Helen licked dry lips, then shrank as he eyed their moist, pink perfection, his expression subtly changing. As she heard the hard intake of his breath, panic clutched her. Her defences where Stein was concerned were growing too weak to risk another attack, especially when her worst enemy was herself!

Backing warily away from him, she murmured, 'Shouldn't we be leaving?'

'Yes.' With a tight-lipped shrug he followed her, closing the bedroom door behind him. A glint of amusement lightened the sombre hue of his eyes as if he understood perfectly her breathless retreat. 'I work hard, you know. I'm sure you don't really begrudge me some reward for my labours.'

If that was all there was to it! At Oakfield, changing for dinner, Helen kept thinking of Stein's remark. A reward was usually given, not taken. How much had he managed to get out of her father, she wondered, while she had been away? Lester had been working up to the day he had taken ill and he had always been astute. He wouldn't have let Stein do him out of anything, she felt sure. Whatever Stein had received it would have been legal, above board, and almost impossible to reclaim. His powers of persuasion being what they were, her father wouldn't have stood a chance.

Helen's pale, doubtful face reflected back from the mirror as she applied a little light make-up. It wasn't the money, she admitted. Money had never been of great importance to her. If she could find the right job, whether with the firm or elsewhere, she would be happy enough with the salary she earned and the satisfaction of being able to do a good day's work. No, what she couldn't face was the thought of Stein being a thief.

That he was intelligent enough to stay within the law was no consolation. Somehow she couldn't bear to contemplate her meeting with Harold Dent. Despairingly she wished she had stayed in France or that she could simply disappear.

The next morning Helen spent in her room, sorting out her new clothes and hanging them away in her wardrobes. She got one of the maids to dispose of the boxes and wrappings. While her cowardly desire to flee hadn't lasted long she did use her room this morning as a kind of refuge. She had no idea where Stein was. He hadn't been in to breakfast and she had guessed he was out riding as he hadn't said anything about going to the office. Suddenly she had wanted to avoid him and retreated upstairs. During dinner, last night, she had felt his mocking glance dwelling on her frequently. They hadn't talked much, but she had sensed in him a cold, cruel triumph which she couldn't explain but which had made her regret her softer feelings towards him. It was obvious he was relishing the situation and not at all dismayed by it—something which strengthened rather than weakened Helen's suspicions.

He wasn't in for lunch either, and she felt resentful that she had to ask where he was. She asked Hilary, the elder of the two maids, but she didn't know. Neither did Olive, the other one. They only knew that he had gone somewhere with Paul in the Rolls.

Helen's annoyance over this was such that when she was served a lunch she considered little less than disgraceful, it gave her the courage to send for Mrs Swinden.

'A slice of tinned meat and a single lettuce leaf is scarcely suitable for a cold day!' she said stiffly when the woman eventually appeared.

Mrs Swinden didn't appreciate being reprimanded. 'Since Mr Maddison isn't here, miss,' she replied coldly, 'I didn't think you'd want anything special.'

'But I give the orders now, not Mr Maddison,' Helen

retorted firmly. 'In future you must consult me.'

'That's not what I've been told,' Mrs Swinden began to argue.

'Well, you know now,' Helen didn't allow her to go any farther, 'and you have adequate assistance. Would you kindly see to it that I get some hot soup and perhaps an omelette?'

She didn't really want either. If Mrs Swinden had apologised she would have forgiven her, but she found the woman's attitude infuriating. She didn't enjoy giving orders. In France she had learnt to obey them, and if she had been able to do that without receiving wages, surely it wasn't beyond the capacity of someone receiving adequate remuneration? Stein had obviously let Mrs Swinden have too much of her own way!

She waited half an hour before a plate of lukewarm soup and a miserable-looking omelette appeared. It was too much! She stormed into the kitchen.

'I'm afraid you'll have to go, Mrs Swinden. Mr Maddison may like to provide you with a reference, but I certainly shan't!'

Mrs Swinden was sitting at the big scrubbed table having coffee with one of the outdoor staff. In front of him was a plate of delicious-looking home-made biscuits. As the man murmured a hurried greeting to Helen and disappeared, Mrs Swinden drew herself up with an injured air, protesting angrily,

'I do my best, Miss Davis, and I've had no complaints until now. I'm sure Mr Maddison is quite satisfied.'

'Well, I'm not!' Helen snapped. 'You can take a week's notice.'

She couldn't remain in the house after this. Running upstairs, she flung on her new mink jacket. It went extremely well with her light slacks and sweater. Brushing back her long, fair hair, she didn't pause to consider the charming picture she made but rushed outside. Wishing she had remembered to ask what had

happened to the smart little car she used to drive, she
made her way on foot towards the village. Her father
had bought it for her a few weeks before she had left; it
must be around somewhere.

She was still feeling angry over Mrs Swinden. How
could her father have come to employ such a woman in
the first place? She wasn't just over-confident, she was
insolent! Good housekeepers might not be easy to find,
but they did exist. Helen felt she would rather manage
on her own than put up any longer with Mrs Swinden.
Stein couldn't possibly object because, regardless of
what Mrs Swinden thought, he had nothing to do with
it.

She reached the village and bought a bar of chocolate
to satisfy the pangs of hunger aroused by her walk.
There was frost on the ground and the air was clear and
bright. With the resilience of youth she began feeling a
little better. She met several people she knew. They
stopped to speak to her, offering sympathy because of
her father. Some of them were curious about Stein, she
could tell, but she managed to parry their rather
devious queries without seeming rude. She accepted a
couple of invitations and it was almost dusk before she
began wandering home again.

She didn't hurry as she wasn't keen to see Mrs
Swinden again. She wouldn't feel comfortable until the
woman was gone. Remembering the household she had
lived in in France, Helen sighed. While Madame Sibour
and her family had suffered a great loss the
fundamental atmosphere in the old house had been a
happy one. There she had cooked and cleaned and
looked after three children, and while she had
sometimes been very tired she had never felt miserable.
It needed children to turn a house into a home, she
thought, wondering if there would ever be any at
Oakfield.

She was almost there when a car pulled up and
Stein's arm drew her in beside him.

'Where have you been?' she exclaimed, too cross to protest at such high-handedness.

'Where have you?' he asked tersely, his eyes slipping too closely over her, she considered.

'Just to the village for some chocolate,' she replied sharply, trying to prevent her pulse moving out of control. He had drawn her into the car so quickly she had lost her balance and fallen against him. For a moment, before she righted herself, her nostrils had been filled with his masculine scent and the vibrations of his heart still seemed to be pounding right through her. It wasn't real, it couldn't be, she told herself. He was as warmly dressed as she was. No pulsebeat could penetrate winter clothing. If she were sensible she would believe it and dismiss such illusions as sheer fantasy.

Her hand trembled as she flicked back her wayward hair. Stein was wearing a formal suit. Had he been lunching with Barbara? 'Where have you been?' she repeated.

'Town,' he said briefly, his eyes on her shaking hand.

She hid it quickly. 'What doing?'

His mouth thinned. 'I'd rather you didn't walk such a distance on your own.'

So he wasn't going to enlighten her, but then he seldom did about anything! 'I need the exercise,' she retorted.

'It was something more than that, I think?' His eyes narrowed on her face.

'Yes,' Helen admitted reluctantly. He had to know some time and she saw no sense in denying it, but she didn't want to discuss it now; Paul might overhear. 'I'll tell you later.'

'Is it something I can look forward to?' Stein asked grimly, as Paul drew up outside the house.

'Perhaps not,' she confessed grudgingly. 'It's about Mrs Swinden.'

'Ah!' he paused enigmatically after following her from the car. 'I might have known.'

She glanced at him sullenly. 'You don't sound very sympathetic.'

He waved Paul off in the direction of the garages. 'I'm afraid I haven't time to listen to your domestic problems at the moment. I have to see someone.'

'Someone coming here?'

'Not to the house,' he replied, with an impatient glance at the darkening sky.

As he strode away Helen noticed how the wind ruffled his dark hair, emphasising the strong lines of his head. She remembered how Barbara had looked at him and felt a flicker of jealousy, then was furious with herself.

Too restless to go inside immediately, she wandered around the back of the house, where she bumped into Paul.

'Do you live here?' she asked in surprise.

'I have a room with one of the gardeners,' he said.

'I thought you would prefer London?'

'I do,' he grinned, 'but I have to be around when the boss wants me.' His smile lingered lazily. 'He's a busy man and can't be kept waiting, you know.'

'He's seeing someone,' Helen muttered, the comment dropping idly from her lips as she concentrated on what Paul had been saying.

'Yes,' Paul unwittingly explained the reason for Stein's hurry. 'Cullan, the gardener I'm with, was telling me there's some trees to come down. One fell across the main road last week and nearly caused a nasty accident.'

Why hadn't Stein told her about it? Helen wondered angrily as she went to find him. She ought to have been consulted. They were, after all, her trees!

When she tracked him down he was talking to a man with a truck at the bottom of the ten-acre field. She knew the trees; they were old and she didn't doubt becoming a danger. If Stein had mentioned them she might have let him deal with the situation. What she didn't appreciate was his arrogant determination to ignore her. He wasn't going to find it easy handing over the reins!

Seeing her coming, he muttered something to the contractor and walked towards her. 'Did you want me for something?' he asked.

Her colour deepened at his distinctly discouraging tone. Did everyone think they could speak to her as they liked? 'Why didn't you tell me where you were going?' she retorted.

'Because I knew you would want to come,' he sighed, 'and I didn't think you were up to it.'

'And I suggest it was because you didn't want me to know what you were doing!' she countered recklessly.

His stony face tightened. 'You aren't going to make a fuss over a few trees, surely?'

She stared at him coldly, then glanced past him. 'Isn't that Charlie Parkinson?' she asked.

'Right first time,' Stein jeered. 'Can you fault him? There's not much he doesn't know about timber.'

'How much is he paying?'

'He's felling them in return for the wood. We've more than we can use up ourselves. There's only about half a dozen, and they're very rotten. They should have been down long ago.'

'Don't dare criticise my father!' she cried.

'Helen!' he snapped, as the contractor gazed towards them curiously. 'I've stood about enough! Are you going in, or do I have to carry you?'

Helen simmered gently all the way through dinner. The whole meal was beautifully cooked and presented, which didn't improve her temper. Mrs Swinden had certainly surpassed herself this evening, in order, obviously, to try and keep her job and make Helen look a fool if she dared complain to Stein.

Stein, not aware of the fiasco in the kitchen, appeared to connect Helen's mutinous face with their argument over the trees, and retired to the study with his coffee.

Helen gave him time to drink it before she followed. She didn't bother to knock. Unless it was a bedroom she refused to knock on any more doors in her own home!

He glanced up from a pile of what she took to be forms and lists and sheets of paper. They were on the desk and he was seated behind it. His glance as he saw Helen was impatient. With a sigh he pushed the papers aside and folded his arms.

'Now what is it?' he asked, his grey eyes expressionless, his face far from encouraging.

'I want to speak to you,' she said coldly, refraining from accusing him of disappearing when he must have known this. 'I told you!'

His dark brows tilted. 'I realise you're still annoyed over the trees, but there doesn't seem anything more to discuss.'

'We never got started,' Helen retorted indignantly, recalling the abrupt way he had overridden her protests and dismissed her. 'There's still more I'd like you to explain about those, but there's something else which is more important.'

Stein frowned, then nodded towards a chair, which she took to be an invitation to sit down. When she shook her head he rose and came round the desk to stand beside her, his eyes narrowing on the thick, shining beauty of her hair.

'I'm listening,' he prompted softly.

Something in his attitude flicked her temper again. She almost said she hoped it wasn't too much trouble! Calming herself with a deep breath, she wished he had stayed behind the desk.

'It's Mrs Swinden. I've given her a week's notice, and I'd rather you didn't interfere. If she approaches you I want you to back me up.'

There was a brief silence while he stared at her blankly. 'What brought this on, might I ask?'

'I don't mind telling you about it,' angrily she lifted

her chin, her eyes flashing like blue jewels in her small flushed face. 'I'm afraid I've never cared for her general attitude.'

'Never?' he interrupted dryly.

'All right!' she snapped. 'I know I've only been home a week, but it doesn't take as long as that to recognise insolence.'

'I've always found her quite pleasant.'

'She would be to you, you're a man!'

Stein's eyes glinted. 'She might be able to teach you a thing or two, if you weren't so prejudiced.'

Helen refused to let him get under her skin. 'I've tried to make allowances. I mean, I realise she hasn't been used to having a mistress.'

His mouth quirked grimly. 'So?'

'She served me a terrible lunch and when I asked for something hot, she gave me cold soup and an omelette I wouldn't have given my worst enemy!'

'So?'

Helen glared at him, wishing he would stop saying that with a patent boredom which indicated he had already lost interest.

'I went to the kitchen and told her she could go!'

'I'm sure she'll forgive you?' he murmured soothingly.

'Forgive me?' Helen gasped. 'You can't be serious?'

'A housekeeper is very difficult to replace,' he pointed out reasonably.

'I don't want to replace her!' Helen all but shouted, her blue eyes fixed stormily on his impassive face. 'Can't you get that into your thick head? The whole lot will have to go in a few weeks, when I sell this place. Until then I'll do the cooking myself!'

'Heaven help me!'

A faint red tinged his cheeks and she didn't stop to wonder if his terse exclamation had anything to do with her cooking. 'You may be wise to ask,' she blazed, 'because I'm not sure if anyone else will? I know I didn't treat my father right, but that had nothing to do with you.' She forgot her remorse over the way she had also treated Stein as she rushed on. 'I won't stand for being ordered about and cheated any longer. God knows how much you manged to steal from my father, but I won't allow you to continue stealing from me!'

'That's enough!' Stein spoke between his teeth as he lunged for her, looking so formidable that Helen was suddenly frightened. She tried to retreat, but he took hold of her shoulders and began shaking her. She could see the veins on the strong muscles of his neck standing out and his eyes momentarily held the blackness of unconcealed rage.

'You'll pay for every insulting word you've uttered!' he snarled.

'Let go of me, you swine!' she gasped, hearing a seam of fragile material tearing under the abuse of his relentless hands. Irrationally, because it was the last thing she was thinking of, she screamed, 'You can pay for a new dress!'

'Getting money out of me for that might be the least of your worries,' he rasped menacingly. 'I'd like to break every beautiful bone in your body. Not before I've had you, of course!'

'That's one ambition you can forget about!' she cried wildly, her eyes still defiant.

Stein stopped shaking her but didn't release her. He bent towards her, menace in the grey eyes. 'I'll have what you've given others. All the men at those mad parties you were so fond of, and in Paris—and God knows where else!'

'You're crazy!' she moaned.

'You will be, before I'm through with you!' His mouth formed a cold sneer. 'You're not indifferent. I could easily make you want me until you were nearly out of your mind.'

She heard the harsh intake of his breath as he dragged her closer, felt the pain of his vice-like grip on her shoulders. Then his arms slid around her in savage possession, while he forced her head back under the violence of his kiss, his lips hot and angry, thrusting her mouth open to a probing invasion she was helpless against. When she struggled his arms merely tightened and she was trapped between him and the desk. She could feel his powerful thighs pulsing against her with a desire he made no attempt to conceal. When he released her, her face was flooded with hot colour and she was trembling.

'Are you through?' she whispered, rubbing a hand over her bruised mouth.

'For the moment,' he nodded coldly but with a certain savagery in his eyes.

'Don't threaten me!' she said hoarsely, trying to measure the distance between him and the door. There was a high flush over his cheekbones and his eyes were glittering fiercely. He seemed almost out of control, and her trembling increased. Every time he touched her she was having to fight harder with herself. She was desperately afraid that if he really tried, she might go up like straw in the wind, fanned by the flames of his physical desire. She needed love, she told herself frantically, not this kind of thing!

Stein was watching her, staring down at her mouth, a glittering expression on his face, almost as though he was mentally plundering it again. 'I'll threaten you all I like,' he muttered. 'And I won't just stop at threats. I have a large sexual appetite, Helen.'

'You're crazy!' she choked, wondering how often she had told him. 'I'll get Harold Dent to throw you out! I don't want you here.'

His eyes hardened as he said with a savage smile, 'You can get alarmed when I don't want you!'

'I'll go to the police!' she cried, her face blazing.

'Whenever you like,' he laughed coldly. 'I'd advise you to wait, though. What will you tell them? That I'm going to seduce you? You'll have a stronger case if you wait until it happens.'

Did he intend pouring mockery over her until she was knee deep in it? 'I hate you!' she snapped furiously. 'You've never done a thing to help anyone but yourself. There's a lot I have to tell Mr Dent!'

'I can't bear to wait,' he sneered. 'The suspense is killing me.'

'I hope something does!' Her eyes were bright with anger. 'I intend ringing Mr Dent's office tomorrow to ask when he'll be back.'

'He hasn't been away,' Stein snapped. 'If you insist I'll arrange for him to come here tomorrow afternoon.'

Helen staggered, and might have fallen if she hadn't been leaning against the desk. Her throat was so tight it hurt her. He was staring at her with icy hostility. If there had been one hint of remorse in his eyes she might have forgiven him. His only emotion appeared to be resentment that she had discovered what he was up to and refused to be a pawn in his game.

She wanted to laugh triumphantly, but somehow she couldn't. A moment ago she could happily have heard Harold Dent denouncing him from the rooftops. Now she couldn't bear to think of it. It wasn't Stein who was going crazy, it was herself!

Determined to strengthen such a ridiculous weakening of her defences, she said stiffly. 'Thank you. I don't actually know if you own any shares in the company, but if it's only a job . . .'

'Shut up!' he cut her off tersely.

'Stein, please . . .!'

Again he refused to listen. 'I'd rather you went to bed, Helen, otherwise you might have even more to regret.' His eyes bored into her, his teeth meeting with a snap. 'I'd advise you not to say another word, not until you've seen your solicitor.'

Upstairs, Helen flung herself on her bed, wishing she could stop shaking. She lay in the darkness trembling, appalled at what had happened. She knew some relief that she was to see Harold Dent at last, but any suggestion that Stein might be proved guilty of criminal offences terrified her. She liked to pretend she hated him and disliked the caresses he forced on her. She seemed to have been fighting him from the moment they had met, but she had a haunted feeling that she didn't really know what her antagonism was about.

When Stein took her in his arms she wanted to cling to him and forget about everything but the demands of her body. She couldn't believe he meant all the terrible things he said to her, yet she shuddered when she thought of the raw hunger she sometimes sensed in him. The dangerous way he lived, his hard arrogance and lack of conscience all repelled her. Yet there were times when, despite recognising the danger, she ached for him. Tonight mightn't she easily have almost precipitated a crisis herself, by responding too passionately to his urgent caresses?

Going to the bathroom, she quickly undressed and took a cool shower. Sick and miserable, she crawled into bed, too torn by unhappiness and worry to sleep. Grief over her father and her present problems overwhelmed her so that she passed most of the hours before dawn lying wide awake with tears streaming down her cheeks.

She must have dozed for an hour after dawn and was startled to find, when she woke and glanced at the clock, it was after nine. A cup of cold tea stood by her bed. She ignored it as she rushed to take another shower. During her short sleep she must have had bad dreams, for her body was wet with perspiration.

Dressing swiftly, she hurried downstairs. She wondered where Stein was and what he was doing. She wanted to know if he intended being around when Mr Dent arrived. He wasn't a coward, but he wasn't altogether predictable.

As she reached the bottom of the stairs he was coming out of the dining-room. Helen hadn't expected to find him so soon, and she felt her face flush, then go pale. He was dressed for business and looked very dark and formidable as he paused and watched her walking hesitantly towards him.

'You—you aren't going to town this morning?' she faltered, the angry words they had exchanged hanging like a pall between them.

'I have to, I'm afraid,' he said grimly. 'I'll see you later.'

His face was drawn, he didn't look as though he had slept much either. Hollowly she wondered if he intended coming back. Her doubts must have shown in her eyes, for he said enigmatically,

'Don't worry, I'm not about to flee the country, my dear, although you might come to wish I had.'

'What can you expect me to think?' she asked, white-faced and bitter. 'After the funeral you told me Harold Dent was away. How do I know when you aren't deceiving me?'

'I thought you needed a few days to get over the shock of your father,' he replied coolly.

Uncertainly she met his inscrutable gaze. How could she tell what part concern for her played in his own interests? Stein appeared to possess a hard, fearless sincerity, yet the worst scoundrels often had honest faces.

'Have you spoken to Harold Dent this morning?' she asked quickly, flushing miserably.

'Yes,' Stein's mouth twisted, 'he'll be here after lunch.'

Helen was waiting when he arrived. He stayed an hour and when he left she could barely find the composure to say goodbye. The solicitor, never having felt so uncomfortable in his life, didn't linger. If it hadn't been for Stein Maddison's insistence he doubted if he would have been here at all, but Mr Maddison wasn't a man one could afford to offend. And of course, at one time Lester Davis had been a valued client, as well as a friend.

Helen didn't leave the library. She rang for Hilary to show Mr Dent out. When the girl returned to say he had gone, she glanced at Helen curiously.

'Can I get you anything, Miss Davis?'

Helen shook her head. She knew she must be white. She was reeling! She waved Hilary away and sat down, her mouth working convulsively as she tried to get a hold of herself. 'Dear God!' she gasped, burying her face in her hands.

Then, as if the agony inside her couldn't be contained any longer, she jumped to her feet and ran from the room. She didn't go upstairs; somehow the house was suffocating her. Without waiting to find a coat, or even a jacket, she ran outside. The only clear thought in her head was to get away. It was important that she was miles away before Stein came home. She couldn't face him!

Gusty showers of sleet came from the east, driven by a wind that was icy cold. It buffeted her slender figure, and before she reached the end of the drive her sweater was almost soaked. As she turned the final corner before the road, a car swept round it, catching her a glancing glow. She landed on the grass verge, not hurt but shaken.

'You little fool!' in a daze she heard Stein's voice as he dragged her inside the car. 'You're making a habit of this!'

'Am I?' She blinked at him, trying to focus. Everything swam before her eyes. She couldn't see his face, but his voice was harsh.

'Where the hell were you going?' he snapped, thrusting her away from him against the seat.

Mercifully she didn't have to find an answer as Paul, suspecting a crisis, put on a spurt. Reaching the house he swiftly opened the car door to let them out, Helen's obvious state of shock providing a chance to prove his ability to react with speed in an emergency.

With an abrupt nod of dismissal, Stein put his arm round Helen, half lifting her into the house. He didn't stop until they reached the library where Hilary was replenishing the dying fire.

He got rid of her as quickly as he had Paul, before she could comment on Helen's bedraggled appearance. The fire smouldered and the room was chilly, despite the central heating. Helen shivered, wondering if she would ever be warm again. Stein's face might have been fashioned from stone. A whimper escaped her white lips as he dumped her unceremoniously in the nearest chair.

'Now you can tell me why you were trying to commit suicide,' he ground out. 'If you'd dashed on to the main road as carelessly as you came round that corner, you wouldn't have stood a chance!'

CHAPTER FIVE

'I WASN'T trying to do anything like that,' Helen whispered.

'Then what were you trying to do?' Stein demanded.

As if he couldn't guess! 'Mr Dent . . .' she began hoarsely.

'Ah, so that's it!' A cruel smile curved the strong lips. 'Given you something of a shock, has he?'

'Why didn't you tell me?' she shivered. She would have given anything for a drink. She looked longingly at the glass of whisky Stein was pouring for himself, but he didn't appear to notice. He didn't offer her anything, not even a cup of tea. Helen reminded herself she wasn't entitled to anything. Nor had she any money to pay for anything.

He swallowed his drink in one go, then poured himself another which he sat down with and savoured slowly. He might have been deliberately taunting her with it. As her staring eyes fixed on it he turned the glass consideringly in his long, steely fingers.

'Why didn't I tell you what?' he asked almost idly.

She caught her breath on a sob. He meant to make her spell it out, and could she blame him? In his position she might have been contemplating slow murder, with every bit as much of the brutal anticipation she could read in his eyes.

'That you own everything.'

'Everything?' One dark brow lifted sardonically.

Helen whispered, too miserable to be angry at such obvious baiting, 'The firm, the house, everything I thought Dad owned. Why did neither of you say anything?'

His eyes flashed coldly on her face. 'Why didn't you

try and work it out for yourself? I'll tell you why!' his voice hardened with contempt as he answered his own question. 'You were too busy jumping to the worst possible conclusions. You decided I was a scoundrel, a liar, a cheat, without any evidence whatsoever. Perhaps I was waiting to see how low I could go, in your estimation, I mean.'

Knowing she had no defence, Helen swallowed painfully. 'I'm sorry, Stein. I had no idea.'

'Or you would have regarded me quite differently. Is that what you're trying to say?'

His cold sarcasm hit her like a blow. If she had known it would have altered everything, she couldn't deny it, but not for the reasons he hinted at, surely? Yet how could she be sure of this? Hadn't she frequently condemned him in her own mind of being all the things he had just stated?

Wretchedly she didn't try to defend herself. 'I thought you were out for what you could get,' she admitted, not attempting to hide her guilt. 'When Mr Dent told me you controlled a group of international companies, I couldn't believe it. But he had proof.'

'Of course you would need that,' Stein retorted derisively. 'That's why I sent for him.'

Dully she asked. 'Why didn't you send for him last week? You did say it was to give me time to recover from the funeral, but I don't think that was the real reason. Not now.'

He didn't argue. 'Perhaps,' he grated, 'I didn't want to be too unkind, not until I was convinced you hadn't changed.'

Blankly she stared at him. 'Changed?'

'From the spoilt little bitch you were when you went away.'

While she flinched from his scorn, Helen knew she had given him every reason to remember her in this light, as this was the impression she must have given. She wasn't sure, even now, exactly why. She had frittered her time away trying to find some relief from her resentment of Stein and her father. But it had been more than that. She had been terrified of what happened to her whenever she got too near Stein. Subconsciously she had been frightened that the hold he appeared to have over her emotions might make her forget everything she imagined him guilty of. He didn't know this, of course, and she would never tell him. It didn't matter now and her only refuge lay in silence. How he would jeer if she were to say, 'I was falling in love with you and thought you were deliberately encouraging me in order to get your hands on my father's money.'

Bleakly she murmured, 'You don't think I've changed?'

'No, I do not!' he snapped harshly. 'Haven't the last few days proved it? You couldn't wait to start throwing your weight about. You tried to dismiss Mrs Swinden and even ordered me out.'

She had, practically. Miserably she looked down at her hands and saw they were shaking. Her clothing was still wet, but nerves and shock were more responsible for the state she was in. Blindly she nodded, unable to deny it. 'I can only say,' she gulped, 'that it might have been fairer to have told me. I can't believe there was any need for such secrecy.'

Stein rose to pour himself another drink, but again didn't offer her anything. He returned to his seat, his movements deliberate, as though he enjoyed keeping her in suspense. Helen watched indifferently as he slowly raised his glass. Somehow she had lost all desire for sustenance of any kind. Even a drink might have choked her.

He surveyed her, his eyes, no warmer than she felt, wandering over her slight, shivering figure. 'Your father asked me not to say anything. It was, in fact, part of our agreement. He didn't want you to know he'd lost everything.'

Harold Dent had mentioned that Lester had owed such huge sums of money he had found it impossible to carry on, but there was a lot the solicitor hadn't explained. He had obviously had no idea Helen hadn't been fully aware of the true situation from the beginning. There was only Stein, and he wasn't making it easy, but she had to know.

She stared at him entreatingly, her eyes huge in her white face. 'How could he expect to keep something like this from me indefinitely? Other people must have known. It couldn't have been any great secret!'

'It wasn't.' Stein's voice was curt and dry. 'If you'd been older and wiser you might have realised. Why do you think Lester kept you in the typing pool?'

'To get experience.'

'Experience, my foot!' Stein muttered, half under his breath. 'It was to keep you in ignorance of the true state of affairs. That was why he made you leave your job.'

Helen's face was a dreadful colour and she trembled afresh as every word Stein uttered seemed to emphasise her own stupidity. When she thought back, there had been odd things, but she had been too dazzled by a future image of herself as head of the firm to take much notice of danger signals. She should have been more observant, but she wasn't unintelligent. If only Stein had given her a hint!

'You can't have been legally obliged to go on helping him to deceive me,' she said.

Stein's mouth tightened. 'I wasn't. The situation happened to intrigue me at a time when I was feeling a trifle jaded.'

'You mean you did it to amuse yourself?'

'Partly,' he allowed. She didn't notice the wary note in his voice. 'Your father was determined to sell only to someone agreeable to keeping all knowledge of his insolvency from you.'

'Surely,' Helen cried incredulously, 'he didn't expect to find anyone willing to take him seriously?'

'There was just a chance he might have succeeded,' Stein said grimly. 'I knew of at least two other companies who were interested enough not to allow a little thing like that to stand in their way.'

'Why did you want the firm?' she asked tonelessly.

'Because of its future potential,' he replied briefly.

Future potential? That could mean anything? Bitterly she gazed at him. 'So you took over the lot?'

'The lot?'

'The firm, this house—my father!' Her voice rose. 'How could he have lost it all? He never mentioned a thing. Do you know how it happened?'

'It didn't happen overnight,' Stein replied curtly, 'He stuck to old-fashioned technology and refused to install new machinery and left too much to other people. The competence, in some cases integrity, of his executive staff left a lot to be desired. When he first found he was getting into difficulties he should have done something then.'

'What could he have done?' Helen whispered.

Stein eyed her ruthlessly. 'If a firm is to be saved something usually has to be done when the rot first sets in. Your father could also have tried to retrench in his personal life. He had expensive—er—hobbies.'

'Hobbies?'

'You must have been aware of it. He stayed in London and went abroad a lot.'

Helen frowned. 'On business.'

'That's one name for it, I suppose,' Stein's eyes held cool derision. 'Some men make pleasure their main business in life.'

She stared at him, horrified at what he seemed to be implying. 'I don't believe you!'

'You don't have to look so stunned,' he snapped. 'In a way your father was a free agent, and you can't criticise him for enjoying the same things you're so fond of yourself. Whatever else he did he didn't neglect you. He did everything he could to make amends. He even considered it a just punishment when you went off and left him.'

Helen felt too bewildered to protest as Stein coldly condemned her. There was too much evidence to dispute what Stein was telling her, but there was still a lot she failed to understand.

'How could I know anything had changed? Dad was still with the firm when you joined it, when you apparently took over, that is. I never guessed.'

'You weren't meant to,' said Stein. 'He carried on working as part of the deal and we found him a position where he could do no harm.'

'In other words,' Helen interrupted bitterly, 'We were living on your charity?'

'If you like,' he shrugged, 'but at least you didn't know. You weren't difficult to fool.'

'Perhaps I wasn't,' she admitted, flushing unhappily. 'But don't forget,' she added with a fraction more spirit, 'that mightn't have been wholly my fault. I was sent here and you were there.'

As if he understood perfectly what she was trying to say, his mouth thinned. 'I wasn't there often, just occasionally.'

'You came home with Dad most evenings.'

'Until you were sick of the sight of me,' he taunted harshly.

She ignored this, not having the nerve to deny it, or able, with his icy eyes fixed on her, to find the courage to agree. 'You frequently slept here,' she muttered feebly.

'But not with you, you made sure of that,' he snarled, 'I wasn't good enough, or you thought I wasn't. How you must be regretting that little mistake!'

'Why did you come?' she persisted, her skin hot but refusing to believe Stein's visits had had anything to do with her. Not now.

'The house was mine,' he shrugged. 'A new acquisition, if you like.'

'Of course,' she nodded dully, 'I forgot. But I didn't know then, did I?'

'It shouldn't have made that much difference,' he said acidly.

'It's funny, isn't it?' she laughed, almost hysterically. 'I objected to you staying in your own house!'

'Do you think I didn't realise?' he mocked harshly. 'I hadn't counted on such undisguised antagonism. It didn't take me long to realise you hated me.'

'Hate's a strong word,' she gulped miserably.

His face darkened. 'You're a girl with strong feelings.'

Was she? Helen's eyes clouded desperately. She didn't want Stein to know what she was like. She didn't even want to acknowledge to herself that her feelings for him were so deep they were often in danger of making her forget everything else. 'I—I don't believe I am,' she murmured weakly.

His mouth twisted derisively. 'Don't say it only happens with me! When I kiss you I can feel the force of them. It's quite exciting, I can tell you. But then,' he jeered coldly, 'I don't suppose I'm the first man to be aware of that.'

She wasn't sure what he was talking about. She did know he was the first man who had ever aroused her to any extent. She swallowed hard as she remembered certain moments, especially since she had come home again. As she lowered thick lashes to hide her revealing expression, she noticed Stein's eyes were quite savage.

Why did she feel the way she did only when he kissed her? she wondered despairingly. He had made it impossible for her to whip up any interest in other men. Hadn't she tried hard enough at those silly parties she had once been to? It had been no use. The outcome had left no room for doubt. In another man's arms she might have been made of wood. Eventually she had given up, resorting to drowning her secret longing for Stein Maddison in too much alcohol and dancing. If she hadn't been successful, no one knew but herself, and no one was likely to know now. Stein was staring at her and she could feel the contempt in his eyes beating into her, even when she had her own closed.

'I think,' she whispered helplessly, glancing at him again, 'you imagine a lot about me that isn't true.'

His mouth curled in a sneer at one corner as he rejected such a suggestion. 'I never have to use my imagination where you're concerned,' he said unpleasantly. 'I know you, Helen, even if I don't like you. You might not realise that what you've given to other men is nothing compared with what you're going to give to me.'

'If it's money you're talking about,' she said hollowly, 'I haven't any.'

'It isn't,' he snapped, 'but it's interesting to know what you amount to financially.'

'I don't have enough to get me to London,' she confessed expressionlessly. 'I'll have to beg a lift.'

'And then?' he enquired suavely.

'I'll find a job.'

His gaze searched her set features narrowly. 'You aren't trained for anything.'

'There's sure to be something,' she retorted, more optimistically than she felt.

'Maybe on the streets you might pick something up?'

Helen's face went a shade whiter and she flinched. His meaning was so clear she wanted to hit him, but she couldn't even afford a sharp reply. Whatever he said, whatever he chose to throw at her by way of insults, she must endure it.

'Why did you let us go on living here?' she groaned, her mind spinning unsteadily back to what she considered the main issue. 'Wouldn't it have been kinder to have turned us out in the beginning?'

Impatience hardened his eyes. 'It was your father's stipulation that you should stay, not mine. In a way I confess it suited me to have someone here looking after the place. At the time I thought I had too many commitments to take up residence here permanently, and there are certain risks involved in leaving a house standing empty.'

'And after I went to France?' she asked flatly.

'I began repairing and rebuilding,' he said coolly.

'The swimming-pool,' she said, colour invading her cheeks as she recalled the comments she had made about it.

'Yes,' the glint in his eyes showed he remembered too, 'that was a new innovation. Useful for entertaining, now that I'm living here most of the time.'

She could imagine gay house-parties with Barbara Bates helping him to amuse his guests. Or maybe he intended getting married. When men spoke of settling down they usually had a wife in mind. She tried to imagine the kind of girl Stein would marry, and felt suddenly degrees colder.

'Did you often stay here while I was away?'

Stein shook his dark head. 'Only occasionally when we had people for the weekend. I found the flat more convenient when I wasn't overseas. Your father saw to everything.'

'And I came back and, as you said, began throwing my weight about.'

He took no notice of her bitterness. 'What there is of it,' he agreed, his eyes running over her with a slighting disparagement.

Her face flamed and she shivered. 'You let me make a fool of myself. I think I hate you!'

Immediately Stein was beside her, lifting her bodily out of her chair, his hands gripping her narrow waist far from gentle. As she fell against him helplessly, he pulled her head back to allow his mouth to descend cruelly and crush her lips under his. The pressure, along with the harsh glitter in his eyes, froze Helen with shock so that she was unable to move.

She hadn't expected he would ever want to touch her

again, not even to satisfy a need for revenge, which was what this assault on her obviously was. She felt the warmth of his hard, male body, his movements deliberate and calculated, imposing his masculine superiority with a strength she found impossible to fight.

His mouth was savage until she became limp to the point of fainting at the pain he was inflicting. Then, with a contemptuous exclamation he thrust her back into the chair.

As she collapsed, shaking, he bent over her, his eyes smouldering with rage. 'Don't ever let me hear you say you hate me again,' he snarled, 'or you know the penalty!'

He looked so murderous her control almost broke. She had thought his anger was going, but it must have been still simmering under the surface. 'Leave me alone!' she gasped, as his furious face came closer and amazingly something inside her yearned towards him.

Abruptly he straightened with a muttered oath, a dark red tinge on his hard cheeks. 'I wouldn't fancy you as you are now,' he mocked. 'You hair's wet and so are your clothes, but I know you aren't as indifferent as you pretend to be. I have a theory that you want me. You were trembling in my arms and you've been used, in Paris, to having a man around. I'm just wondering how long it's going to be before you come begging?'

Horrified, Helen stared at him, fright and anger bringing a hectic flush to her white face. 'If you imagine I'm staying here to provide you with free entertainment, you're wrong!' she gasped. 'I'm leaving as soon as I get packed. I'll hitch a ride.'

'You'll do nothing of the kind!' he snapped savagely. 'Attempt to leave and I'll have you hunted down like a thief. And believe me, Miss Davis, I have enough money and influence in high places. You wouldn't stand a chance!'

As she shrank from the menace almost visibly

emanating from him, Helen's thoughts churned frantically. Threats were easy. Men threatened in order to wield power. It was merely bluff, only effective against those easily intimidated. She was filled with self-contempt for not having the courage to defy him as she heard herself protesting weakly, 'Surely you don't really want me to stay?'

'How many times do I have to tell you,' he rapped, 'I'm not finished with you yet. When the day comes that I'm satisfied you can leave as soon as you like, but not until then. If you're tempted to try and run, I'd advise you to think again. You owe me so much that apart from anything else I could have you arrested for non-payment of debts.'

Helen gasped, going very white. What was he saying? A terrible sense of fear and desolation swept over her, but, other than being conscious of this, she didn't seem able to work anything out. Her mouth was dry and her head ached. She knew she must be staring at Stein like a frightened rabbit, but she didn't know how to reply.

He turned away, as if the sight of her offended him. Setting down his empty glass, he said curtly, 'We can discuss the matter of your debts another time. I have a dinner appointment in town and don't want to be late.'

Helen struggled to her feet, swaying but able to stand. It was dark and still raining, she could hear the rain against the windowpanes. She felt suddenly very much alone. Stein hated her and was determined to make her pay for everything she had done, but she couldn't believe he would really hurt her. In the heat of anger people often said things they didn't mean. Once Stein had had time to cool down he might change his mind and be only too willing to let her go.

'Do the staff know you won't be in for dinner?' she asked automatically. Then, remembering, she flushed and apologised stiffly. 'I'm sorry, Stein. I forgot it's none of my business any more.'

'I told Mrs Swinden, this morning,' he replied

shortly, 'I also informed her that you'd made a mistake and I wanted to retain her services.'

The deliberate way he came out with this caused Helen to sway beneath another wave of humiliation. Unhappily she bowed her head. Mrs Swinden would be triumphant, but did it matter? What did anything matter now? Something slid down Helen's cheek to her mouth and her tongue, in unconscious reaction, slipped out to catch it. She was stupidly surprised to realise it tasted salty and was a tear. Suddenly terrified that Stein might discover she was crying, she lowered her head still farther.

'I don't think I want any dinner,' she gulped.

'You'd be lucky to be offered anything,' he said curtly, and left her swiftly, without another glance.

Helen trailed upstairs after him, as he went to change. She could have stayed where she was until he had gone, but she didn't relish one of the maids finding her upset.

In her room, because she felt so terribly cold, she stripped off her wet clothes and ran a hot bath. The bathroom, like her bedroom, had been newly decorated. A luxurious coloured suite had been installed, with toning tiles on the walls and marble ones on the floor. Mirrors lined one wall, giving Helen a full-length view of herself as she stepped from the bath. Before wrapping herself in a huge, fluffy towel, she caught a quick glimpse of a girl of average height, very slender, with full breasts, narrow waist and long, beautiful legs. Ordinary, she thought, with an indifferent shrug, failing to notice anything special. Bitterly she concentrated, instead, on the new décor. When she had returned from France she had regarded it merely as a sign of her father's increasing affluence and wept that he hadn't lived to enjoy it.

Despairingly she returned to her room and flopped on the bed. Never again would she take anything for granted. She still felt stunned and numb from what she had just learnt. Drawing a ragged breath, she tried to envisage what it was going to be like when the numbness wore off and the real pain began. Already she was beginning to feel she had been ripped to pieces.

Like a reel of broken film, thoughts passed disjointedly through her mind. So—the firm had gone bust. Nothing extraordinary about that in times of recession. What was extraordinary, and hurt most, was that her father hadn't told her about it. If he had, whatever reason he might have given, she couldn't have been more hurt than she was now. Stein had hinted that Lester had gone bankrupt because he had been both careless and extravagant. So had Mr Dent.

It was probably true, she admitted dully, recalling things which had struck her as odd at the time. Phone calls from women who'd refused to give their names. It hadn't happened often enough to make her really curious, but it was something she remembered now with a frown. And Lester had been furious when the manager of a famous casino had contacted her at Oakfield to ask if she could tell him where he was. This all made sense now, in view of what Stein had said and Mr Dent's delicately discreet hints of the afternoon. But, like Stein, he had insisted that the true cause of Lester's downfall had been his inability to keep abreast of times.

Helen sighed as she thought of her father's constant moans that she hadn't been born a boy. He might have been trying to use her as an excuse for his own deficiencies, she realised sadly, filled with pity for him, despite the way he had made her suffer. Obviously, for some reason, when the firm collapsed, he had been unable to face her knowing he was a failure. According to Lester it was only women who failed. Perhaps that was why he had merely amused himself with them instead of marrying again, and why, until the last few months, he had almost entirely rejected his daughter.

Helen had no idea how long she sat on her bed

thinking of her father and trying to sort something out of the chaos he had left behind. If she was glad of one thing it was that she felt no bitterness towards him. She was grateful that she could still remember him with affection even if it didn't help in solving her immediate problems. She was still trying to decide what to do when Hilary brought her a tray.

'Mr Maddison rang from London.' She gazed at Helen curiously. 'He said you weren't feeling well and I had to bring your dinner up here.'

Helen thanked her, feeling surprised. She wondered why Stein had bothered. When he had last spoken to her she had got the impression he wouldn't care if she starved. He must have guessed she would stay in her room.

'Can I get you anything else?' Hilary asked.

'Oh, no, thank you.'

'Well, you can always ring.' Hilary's brown eyes wandered enviously over Helen's long, luxuriant hair. 'I do wish my hair was like yours, miss!' she burst out, 'It's so thick and glossy it looks like silk. Mrs Swinden thinks you must spend a fortune on it.'

'Well, I don't,' Helen said dryly, wishing she had a fortune, if only to repay Stein! 'I suppose I'm just lucky,' she managed to raise a faint smile, 'I have it cut, that's all, and it grows again very quickly.'

As Hilary departed, her eyes still envious, Helen glanced at the tray she had left with a complete lack of interest. She had been reluctant to ask Hilary for some aspirin, then suddenly remembered there was some in the bathroom cabinet. After finding them and swallowing two with a glass of water, she lay down and began pondering again, although her head felt like it might explode any minute.

She hadn't heard Stein go out, nor did she hear him come in, but when a noise woke her, hours later, she decided it might have been his car door closing. It must have been Paul dropping him off on the forecourt below. When Stein drove himself he usually took the car straight into the garage and was much quieter. Dismally she wondered who he had been dining with, whether it had been Barbara or someone equally glamorous.

Wearily she rubbed a hand over her face. Her eyes were damp and felt hot and sore, as if she'd been crying in her sleep. She realised she must have fallen asleep, despite having so much on her mind. She had been going impatiently over everything that had happened during the last eighteen months, sure that something was still eluding her.

And suddenly, in the darkness, she knew with a sense of shock what it was. Once more she found herself reeling. Before she had fallen asleep she had been concentrating on finding a way out of her present predicament. When no immediate solution had presented itself, apart from running away, she had been distracted enough to have overlooked one of the most important issues—the one she had known subconsciously was there but which she had been unable to pinpoint. If her father had still owed money after selling the firm, where had her pocket money and dress allowance come from afterwards? There had also been her beautiful sports car and the five thousand pounds he had sent to France—not to mention the expensive clothes she had recently bought in London.

Had Lester borrowed from Stein? Almost in tears again, Helen smothered an anguished whimper. It must have been Stein, because who else would have loaned him anything? No one in their right mind would have done it, considering the circumstances. And if she owed Stein all this money, no wonder he was threatening to have her arrested if she tried to escape!

She had to find out for sure. An overwhelming sense of panic pushed everything else from her mind. Without bothering to fling on more than a light robe, she hurried straight to his room.

Pushing open the door, she stumbled so badly she nearly fell through it. Stein looked as if he hadn't been many seconds in bed. His chest was bare, but a blanket and sheet covered his legs. One hand was raised towards the switch above his head as if he was just about to put out the light.

When he saw Helen he jerked upright, swinging his feet to the floor. 'What the devil?' he exclaimed, cursing sharply beneath his breath as she almost flung herself at him.

'Stein!' she gasped incoherently, raising wild blue eyes to his grim, startled face. 'You have to tell me! Where did all the money come from?'

'What money?' he snapped, searching her stricken features as she fell by his side, with eyes which showed visible signs of tiredness. 'For God's sake, Helen!' he removed her clutching hands from his arms, holding her still, 'What is this? I've had a long day and don't feel up to hysterics. I can't think of anything that couldn't have waited until morning. Unless,' he taunted, 'you at last want to come to bed with me?'

'Can't you stop making silly remarks?' Helen cried, too disturbed to think what she was saying.

'I'm sorry,' Stein jibed smoothly, 'I imagined it was the kind of invitation a woman was after when she came to a man's bedroom at this hour.'

Helen flushed when, as though to emphasise his mocking words, his hands slid under her robe to tighten on her shoulders. His fingers moving on her bare skin began penetrating the frozen state of shock she was in. As her heart beat faster, she wished desperately that she wasn't as responsive to his slightest touch. She wished she wasn't so sure he knew it!

The tension in the room mounted until she could actually feel it altering her breathing. Helplessly her eyes wandered, coming to a jolting halt on Stein's bare chest. It was the first time she had ever seen him like this and her eyes darkened at the wholly sexual impact.

She had known he was no weakling, but she hadn't guessed at the expanse of firmly muscled flesh or the solid width of his shoulders.

'Are you trying to make me believe you've never seen anyone like me before?' he taunted. 'It's a pity I didn't leave off my pyjama trousers—I don't usually wear them.'

'That's a hateful thing to say!' she whispered, hating the heat that flooded her. Sobs rose to her throat while she strove to be calm. Hoarsely she tried to explain the real reason for her visit, but her voice suddenly failed, which gave him another chance to bait her.

'If you think you can buy your freedom by coming here, tonight, you're making a mistake,' he rasped. 'I'll have you when I'm good and ready, not before. Don't imagine you can wipe out what you owe me in a brief half hour. Your punishment is going to be slow and painful, not something you're going to be able to forget in a hurry.'

'You must be out of your mind!' she cried, finding her voice at last, even if she scarcely recognised it.

'Not quite,' he retorted, obviously quite unmoved by the fear clearly visible behind her defiance, 'But it might do you no harm to think so. We have a lot to look forward to.'

'But why?' Helen whispered, so shaken and bewildered she could think of nothing but his threats. 'I'm aware I neglected my father, but it wasn't intentional and I don't believe he bore me any real animosity. As for you and me,' she choked, 'if we've never had a great deal in common that's surely not something I have to be punished for!'

She saw his mouth go hard while his eyes smouldered savagely and a nerve jerked briefly in his cheek. Panic rose up inside her as he looked as if he was remembering a lot he would like to have strangled her for. As his hands slid around her slender neck and his thumb found the racing pulse in her throat, she wondered apprehensively if he was actually going to do it. Then the pressure eased and he merely said harshly, 'It amused you to treat me like dirt.'

Helen's lips trembled. Stein had told her this before. He seemed determined she shouldn't forget it. Of course some of the things she had accused him of had been unforgivable, and he wasn't exactly the forgiving kind. She didn't attempt to turn away, bearing the contempt of his stare as bravely as she could. She had a lot to make up for, but Stein wasn't making it easy. She didn't know where to begin.

His eyes flared darkly as he read her confused thoughts. 'You aren't the only one who's ever tried to humiliate me, Helen, although it hasn't happened in years. Long ago I acquired the knack of dealing very effectively with those who decided I needed taking down a peg or two.'

'But you still don't like opposition from women?'

'I don't have it from women,' he replied derisively. 'You're the first—you can believe it.'

This Helen didn't doubt. She remembered how at parties, before she went away, women had flocked around him. Since coming back, she had only seen him with Barbara, and she had looked ready to obey his every command without the slightest protest. God knew how many others there were, she relected bitterly, ready to commit hara-kiri for him. Once she had thought he had eyes only for Helen Davis. Now she could laugh at her own stupidity. Stein had simply been amusing himself until, surprisingly, the novelty of her rejection began getting under his skin. It must have festered like a sore during the year she had been in France, and he was determined to use any means he could find to cleanse himself of it!

'Don't you think you'd be wiser just to throw me out and forget about me?' she asked bleakly.

CHAPTER SIX

IN the lamplight Stein's eyes glinted angrily, making Helen shiver again. She must never forget he was capable of reprisals far beyond her powers of retaliation. And, physically, he was more than a match for her delicate strength. She didn't believe any woman would be able to stand up to him.

'You'd like that, wouldn't you?' he muttered. 'A quick, clean break. No, my dear Helen, I intend keeping you at Oakfield until you come crawling on your knees saying you're sorry.'

'You wouldn't be content with just that,' she whispered, judging from the extreme hardness of his expression.

'You're damned right I wouldn't,' he snapped. 'I'm going to make you pay in sweat and tears for a long time to come.'

When he spoke of making her pay it started a chain of reaction in her mind. 'Stein!' she gasped distractedly. 'That's what I came to see you about—repaying you all that money!'

'What—money?' he asked flatly.

His glance was wandering slowly over the tender curves of her slender figure, clearly outlined under her thin night attire. In his eyes lay the kind of desire she always shrank from.

Her throat went dry. Like someone half drunk she began reeling everything off. 'The five thousand I asked for when I went to France. My pocket money after I left the firm. My car, the clothes I bought the other day in London. Where did it all come from?'

Despite the broken notes in her voice, Stein appeared to follow her very well. His mouth thinned cruelly. 'I

95

thought you'd never ask. Where do you think it came from?'

Helen shivered, a sudden faintness coming over her. The room darkened, she felt sick. She forced herself to look at him and there wasn't a vestige of pity in his face. 'If my father was practically bankrupt, it must have been you.'

'Yes. Your father didn't have a penny left,' he said frankly. 'In fact, I paid off his remaining debts.'

Colour crept under her skin at his contemptuous tone. 'Why?' she asked, her eyes anguished.

He shrugged indifferently. 'I didn't miss it. And I believed he might be able to pay me back. It didn't amount to all that much.'

She glanced down, feeling terribly chilled. 'When he tried to borrow money for me why didn't you refuse?'

Stein's mouth tightened impatiently. 'If I hadn't obliged someone else would have, and I might only have had to rescue him from the clutches of some disreputable money lender. He was determined to get it from somewhere, and perhaps it amused me to see how far you would go.'

'And now you have me in your clutches,' she retorted bitterly.

'That's about it,' he agreed silkily, 'although I wouldn't have put it quite so dramatically.'

'Whichever way one puts it,' Helen cried wildly, 'it amounts to the same thing!'

His face darkened. 'I realise you meant to sell up here and return to Paris, and I'm sorry if you're feeling frustrated, but there's no way you can escape. You've done wrong and I'm going to see you pay for it.'

His grey glance ruthlessly searched her face, seeing the helpless pallor, the shadowed eyes and trembling, unhappy mouth. 'Co-operate,' he said thickly, suddenly drawing her closer, 'and one day I might let you go. But fight me and you could soon wish you were dead!'

Helen closed her eyes as she was drawn against his

hard, muscled thighs. His harsh words washed over her, his gaze full of such burning intensity that she didn't doubt he meant everything he said. She wondered if he had been drinking, but there was no smell of alcohol on his breath. 'Oh, God!' she moaned.

He drew a sharp breath. 'Don't push me too far,' he warned. 'Remember I haven't started yet.'

'I have to keep my self-respect,' she choked, trying to defy him. It was a message for herself as well, as her heart began accelerating crazily.

'Self-respect!' he laughed harshly. He didn't have to tell her he considered this something she had already lost.

Helen closed her eyes and shuddered against him as she felt the brush of his mouth. The fleeting touch of his kiss sent fever flooding along her veins and her whole face became suffused with colour. The shock she had suffered, her nearness to a complete breakdown, seemed no barrier to the feelings he aroused. As his hands caressed her she tensed, but was unable to resist her own desire to be as close to him as possible.

She wanted to feel his mouth against hers, and a long sigh of hunger escaped her parted lips. He might threaten until she hated him, but never again would she be able to deny that there was something between them. In an incredible way, for surely he was responsible for it, being in his arms seemed to relieve the terrible sense of unhappiness which had beset her for days, reaching its dreadful culmination that afternoon. Just being near him relieved the frightening sensation of being alone. Instead of pulling back, she curved herself tightly to his hard, male body, breathing so fast she knew he must hear it.

His mouth poised above hers, Stein watched her ruthlessly, his eyes not missing a thing. As her eyelashes fluttered helplessly his lips touched her cheek and she murmured his name.

'Stein,' she whispered. 'Oh, please . . .!'

In a daze her arms crept round his neck. She was in such turmoil she scarcely knew what she was doing. For a moment she felt his mouth harden, then he withdrew, leaving her in a state of chill disappointment.

'Are you ready to beg yet?' he asked coldly.

'No!' she gasped with the first breath she could find, wondering if this was part of the torture he was devising. Burning with humiliation, she tried to bury her hot face in the hands he had wrenched from the back of his neck, to prevent him seeing how vulnerable she was.

He didn't allow her any form of retreat. Ruthlessly he thrust her hands aside to lift her chin, crushing the protests from her lips with his mocking mouth. 'You will,' he promised, under his breath.

'But why?' Helen heard herself gasping tremulously.

'Because you're mine,' came back the answer, without hesitation.

Her heart racing unsteadily, she twisted futilely in his grasp, terrified of his insistence. 'You don't own me!' she cried apprehensively. 'I might owe you a lot, but that doesn't give you the right to do as you like with me!'

Her unceasing defiance snapped the control Stein was keeping over his temper. His hard fingers were suddenly biting into her shoulders and her alarmed glance saw that the grey eyes were darkening almost to black. She recognised too clearly the anger blazing in them, and her body began to tremble.

'Stein——' she began.

'I refuse to argue,' he cut her off tersely, reading her mind easily as he stared at her. 'We've been over all this before. You know as well as I do that no amount of talking can alter anything.'

Somehow she couldn't leave it. 'We've scarcely discussed the money you loaned me,' she said desperately. He was still holding her so she couldn't move, but in spite of the pain she didn't want to, not until she made another attempt to make him understand. Otherwise she might never get her freedom. 'I wasn't aware of the true circumstances or I wouldn't have taken a penny!'

One of his hands returned to her chin and, although she shrank from him, he bent to trace a taunting path along her cheek to her ear, his mouth softly tantalising her heated skin. 'Could you prove you were ignorant of the true circumstances?' he drawled sarcastically. 'I suggest you turned a blind eye to what was going on in order to continue leading a life of leisure.'

Beads of perspiration broke out on her temples. 'That's not true!' she gasped.

He watched her intently and she began feeling half demented by his probing grey eyes which seemed to be eating her up. Was he trying to lay her soul bare? she wondered hysterically. Was he searching for indisputable evidence of her guilt?

'A dishonest person,' he snarled, 'often doesn't recognise the difference between borrowing and stealing.'

Helen shivered, frantically moistening suddenly dry lips. He had her trapped, she could see. She must owe him thousands, not to mention the debts he had paid off for her father. She couldn't be sure if he would sue her, but, morally, he had her in a cleft stick. If she refused to do exactly as he said, the outcome might be worse than she could ever imagine. She could see it in the glinting harshness of his eyes, had felt it in the cruelty of his hands and mouth. He was consumed by a thirst for revenge which had to be assuaged. She doubted if he would ever trust her again, but she had to obey him and endure his castigation. She would do anything willingly, all but one thing. Her heart pounded as she prayed he wouldn't ask that of her.

She moved her head back with a jerk as his mouth twisted and he began kissing her again, as if cynically amused by her too transparent thoughts but unheeding of them. This time his kisses were demanding and urgent and she tried to prevent her lips parting in response, her body from arching against his. She had to get away from him! She hoped, if she persisted, he might lose interest and send her to bed. 'You can't believe I knowingly took your money?' she choked, when he allowed her to breathe.

'Don't you ever give up?' he snapped impatiently. 'It might be a good idea if you asked yourself some of the questions you're asking me. The answers you find might surprise you.'

Would they? Trembling, she searched her mind, attempting to do as he suggested. Why hadn't she suspected something was wrong? She had to admit it didn't seem possible that she had remained entirely ignorant of what was happening to her father. If she hadn't been so busy fighting her feelings for Stein, mightn't she have noticed a lot more?

'I can't prove you're wrong,' she said despondently. 'There are things you don't understand.'

'Never mind,' Stein's voice came falsely soothing, 'if you can't settle your debts in the ordinary way, you will in another.'

Helen stiffened as his hands began caressing her intimately, clearly indicating his exact meaning. If she hadn't wholly believed in his threats before she did now.

'You can't be serious!' she cried angrily, a hot flush staining her cheeks.

His grip tightened, forcing a low cry from her. 'I think you ought to know, Helen, I've never been more serious in my life. I intend having you, and you must have realised by now that I usually get what I want in the end.'

'However low you have to stoop to achieve your ends,' she exclaimed unwisely.

He didn't notice the panic driving her. His face darkened, concentrating on her derision. 'Don't ever say anything to me like that again!'

'What do you expect,' she retorted, dredging up her last drains of defiance, 'when you threaten and bully all the time? You use your strength to achieve what you never could otherwise!'

For a moment he stared at her, a muscle jerking in his cheek. As her eyes flashed there was an answering flash in his. 'You're either a fool or a very brave woman,' he said softly.

'I realise I'm not the kind of woman you admire,' she returned hotly.

'What's that supposed to mean?'

'You prefer women like Barbara,' she said coldly.

His eyes narrowed, his glance still intent. 'Ah, yes, Miss Bates,' he smiled. 'So you've noticed how nice she is?'

'I've noticed she looks very willing!' she said bitterly.

'So will you be, before I'm through with you,' he assured her softly. 'There's no need to be jealous.'

'You can't be serious?' she gasped.

'You refuse to believe I am—about anything,' he said curtly. 'Perhaps it's time I stopped talking.'

Before she could move he was lifting her on to the bed, changing his own position to lie down beside her. If she hadn't been so drained and exhausted beneath her fleeting bravado she might have found the strength to fight him. As it was, her struggles lasted only a few moments before being completely suppressed by his weight.

'Have you had enough?' he rasped, as she lay panting under him. 'I won't pretend I intend treating you any better than you once treated me, but I thought you would have the sense to know when you're beaten.'

As far as Stein was concerned she had known she was beaten a long time ago, only she'd had too much pride and too little sense to admit it. She moaned weakly as his mouth searched and found hers and his long, supple fingers tightened their hold on her.

'Open your mouth,' he ordered, his breath searing her lips.

Desire flared up inside her and she obeyed immediately. Helplessly she found herself responding as he began kissing her more deeply than he had ever done previously. Her soft lips moved under his as she began kissing him back, her body arching feverishly to his increasing demands. She was beyond thinking sensibly any more. The blood was singing in her ears and she heard his swift intake of breath as she moved against him. There was an ache in the bottom of her stomach which she sensed only Stein could satisfy, and suddenly she knew she wanted him to make love to her. She had never wanted to belong to a man before, but she did now.

When he thrust her away from him she felt cold and bemused by his abrupt rejection. He rolled on his back and got to his feet, reaching for a heavy silk dressing-gown.

Helen opened dazed eyes, the effort almost beyond her, and stared at him. He was shrugging his powerful shoulders into the black silk robe. He tied the belt before turning to look at her again.

'Go back to your room,' he snapped. 'I don't want a woman who's trying to buy her freedom the only way she knows how.'

She managed to get to the edge of the bed, her face burning, but she had to wait a moment, until the strength returned to her shaking limbs, before she could get any farther.

'You said there was only one way,' she whispered.

'Yes,' Stein admitted furiously, 'but I'd be a fool if I didn't realise your attitude's all wrong.' He moved closer, his face coming within range of the bedside light, so hard and cruel she scarcely recognised it. His mouth contorted in self-derision. 'I may be a fool, but I want your mind as well as your body—and both together. I want to hear you say you can't live without me, there'll be no half measures. And nothing's going to happen so quickly that it will be over before you have time to realise what it's all about.'

It wasn't soothing speculating over what new tortures Stein was about to devise, and Helen fell asleep wondering if she was going out of her mind. In the morning she felt she had just closed her eyes when he was in her room, shaking her.

'Join me in the kitchen in five minutes,' he commanded, as she gazed at him, only half awake, her expression compounded of fear and bewilderment.

'Why?' she managed to ask.

'You're going for a swim,' his tone of voice challenged her to refuse. 'I'm tired of seeing you creeping round like a ghost. Even when I thought you owned the place you looked only half alive. I want the woman you were, Helen, not the shadow of her you appear to be.'

'What can you expect,' she breathed in a daze, 'when I've just lost my father?'

'That happened over eighteen months ago.'

'You never forget, do you?'

Stein's face tightened as he stared at her bare shoulders. 'If you don't get some clothes on you might be surprised at what I can forget,' he retorted enigmatically.

When she joined him in the kitchen it was still dark. 'It's only half past six,' she said, glancing at the clock disbelievingly. 'Why drag me out at this hour?'

'Once, Helen, the majority of people in the country were up before this hour, and I thought I explained the purpose of the exercise upstairs?'

She stared at the two cups of tea he was pouring. Her head ached and so did her legs. 'I don't know that I feel like swimming.'

'Well, isn't that a pity!' He spooned a liberal helping of sugar into both cups, pushing one towards her. 'Drink that—it will put some energy into you. You've

had it too easy in France. Too much sex and lying
around in the sun.'

Helen didn't answer. When Stein stated anything as
decisively he would never believe he was wrong, and her
throat felt so sore she couldn't be bothered to argue this
morning. 'At least there was enough sunshine,' she
muttered dully, as her throat eased with a gulp of hot
tea.

'A lot can be achieved without it,' he said harshly,
taking her arm and steering her out of the back door.

The path from the house to the pool was well lighted
and there was no one around. The air was freezing and
Helen shivered, wishing she had worn a warmer coat. A
few stars twinkled overhead while, from the direction of
an old ruined tower, some distance from the house, an
owl hooted. In some woods not far away another
answered, the sound echoing eerily across the space
between. Usually Helen loved the owls and pigeons and
other birds that lived around Oakfield and she
wondered why, this morning, she failed to appreciate
them. It wasn't only her limbs that seemed frozen, it
was her heart.

In the huge barn where Stein had installed the pool it
wasn't much warmer than it was outside. Helen thought
she would rather die than complain, but she could whip
up no enthusiasm. As she stood on the edge of the pool,
staring down into it, she saw Stein was already in the
water. He was obviously an expert, judging by his
powerful strokes which were bringing him swiftly from
the far end of the pool towards her.

She moved uncomfortably in her bikini without
actually feeling selfconscious. In France many girls
didn't even wear as much, although she had never,
herself, gone in for nude bathing. Dully, as Stein
approached, she began braiding her long hair out of the
way at the back of her head, wishing she had
remembered to bring a bathing cap. She didn't often
use one, but it might have been better than getting her

hair wet when she didn't feel so good.

Stein didn't ask her to join him. When she made no move to do so he simply got out and threw her in. Picking her up in his arms, holding her tightly against his hard wet body, he strode to the top of the pool and threw her in at the deep end.

The shock of the cold water gave Helen such a fright she cried out. Why had he done such a thing? He was always so impatient with her. Remembering the days when his patience had been never-ending, she smothered a sob. Sinking a little way, she instinctively righted herself and shot back to the surface. If he was just having fun, she admitted she might have enjoyed it if she had been feeling better.

She was breathless, but she saw he was laughing. She was startled to see so much warmth in his face. Her heart felt suddenly incredibly lighter as she began thinking he had forgiven her. It seemed a long time since she had seen him looking at her like that.

With the beginnings of a tentative smile on her lips she swam a little further, until she could lift herself out. It was then that she received a rude awakening as Stein crouched derisively over her and pushed her straight back in again.

Too late she realised he had merely been coaxing her to return to his side. Unable to save herself, this time she sank to the bottom like a stone. Stein must have jumped in after her, for she saw him near her in the water. His arms lifted, as if in remorse, to help her, but past resisting such an opportunity, she clenched a fist and hit him furiously on the side of his dark head.

It must have hurt, because she heard a muffled exclamation as he grasped her savagely, hauling her against him. Her hair floated on the water and he grabbed a handful of it to jerk her head over his arm. Before she knew what he was doing, his other hand was supporting her back and she caught a glimpse of the quick anger on his face as he began kissing her mercilessly, until she thought she would choke.

Her lips were crushed against her teeth, she could feel them piercing the sensitive skin, but he easily controlled her when she tried to push him away. He held her closely with only enough room between them to allow his hands free access to what seemed every part of her. They floated slowly towards the shallow end, where Stein's feet hit the bottom and he pulled her full length against him, his legs firmly entwining hers when again she tried to wriggle frantically free of him.

Helen's heart was racing and she moaned, soft, shuddering breaths shaking her. His long fingers played over her, stroking and tormenting until her whole body felt on fire. The heat sweeping through her, combined with the coldness of the water, had a curiously erotic effect. She could feel his whipcord muscles beneath her hot hands, and suddenly she found herself clinging to him, her hands beginning to creep round his neck.

Sensing the danger of this, she gasped against his punishing mouth, 'Will you let go of me, you beast!'

He lifted his head a mere fraction, his eyes still smouldering. 'I'll teach you to hit me, you vicious little brat!'

Helen shivered, her eyes brilliant, her face flushed. Staring at him, she burst out bitterly, 'You shouldn't have thrown me in!'

He bent his head to begin kissing her again, then suddenly paused. 'No,' he agreed shortly, 'that was a mistake, but if I hadn't thrown you in you might have been still standing there thinking about it. I didn't mean you any harm.'

'The way you did it didn't do me any good!'

He shrugged and to her surprise lifted her swiftly out of the water, back to the tiled surrounds. 'If you didn't defy me so much I might not react in a way you don't like,' was all he said.

'You can't expect me to go along with everything you suggest,' she muttered, sweeping the wet hair back off her face, trying to keep her eyes averted from the strength of his tall, lean body.

'I don't make idle suggestions.' His jaw tightened as he looked at her steadily. 'This morning's was for your own good, whatever you choose to think. You look as though a whiff of wind might blow you away, and swimming's one of the finest exercises you can get.'

'I got plenty of exercise in France,' Helen retorted. 'I don't need your help to keep fit.'

Grimly he hauled himself up beside her. 'I could easily wring your lovely neck,' he murmured idly.

She watched the water running off him back into the pool. Her eyes rounded with fear as the savage expression in his eyes made her suddenly nervous. 'Don't you think you've done enough?' she whispered.

He laughed mirthlessly. 'I told you last night, I haven't even started.'

Helen felt as if a giant hand was slowly squeezing the breath out of her, as something at last convinced her he meant every word he said. He was possessive and ruthless and might never let her go until he was convinced she was sorry for all the wrong she had done. Fighting him was no answer. It wouldn't be easy to be humble all the time, but at least she could try. At the moment she didn't feel she had the strength to be anything else.

'I'm sorry, Stein,' putting out a hand, she touched him tremulously, 'I know I've done wrong and I'll try and make amends. I'm willing to stay here or go away, whatever you like.'

He withdrew, throwing off her hand impatiently as his eyes narrowed. Dully Helen realised he didn't trust her, and probably never would. His breath rasped, his eyes regarding her icy, while his mouth thinned. 'I haven't decided what I'm going to do with you,' he said harshly, 'but one thing you can believe. I won't let you go. I wish I could.'

Afterwards Helen tried to make sense of what Stein

had obviously stated in anger. She wasn't foolish
enough to imagine she had any power over him and
came to the conclusion that his brief, bitter words
before leaving her at the pool had more to do with the
punishment he felt compelled to mete out because of
Lester than because of himself.

She didn't see Stein again after they returned to the
house. From her room she heard a car draw up outside
the front door and drive away. She presumed it was
Paul, taking him to London.

She had intended asking Stein at breakfast if he could
find her something to do. The thought of being idle all
day filled her with dismay. While she had believed she
owned Oakfield she had had plenty to occupy her mind,
if nothing else. She almost cringed with shame as she
recalled the hours she had spent going around the house
and grounds trying to calculate how much money Stein
had squandered. No wonder he couldn't forgive her!

To discover she had neither property nor money was
frightening but might not have seemed so bad if she had
had a job to stop her thinking about it. There was
nothing she could do here. She could imagine what Mrs
Swinden would say if she offered to help in the house. If
Stein hadn't already told them, she wondered how long
it would be before the staff discovered her true
position? People living at close quarters with each
other, whatever their capacity, had a peculiar knack of
discovering exactly what was going on.

She had been going to plead with Stein to help her to
find something. She had looked after children in France
and would be willing to do this kind of work again. Or,
if he wouldn't allow that, she had hoped he might offer
her her old job back in the firm. The firm must now be
incorporated with his other companies but would still
be there, and if necessary she could travel to town with
him each day.

She had to do something. She couldn't continue
living on his charity, she didn't want to get any deeper

in his debt. She didn't even have much left for the small, essential items it was necessary to purchase from time to time. With all these thoughts churning feverishly in her mind she had gone upstairs to dry her hair before tackling him, but in her room she began feeling really ill.

Not even a hot shower revived her, and she was still sitting shivering as she heard Stein depart. So much for her immediate plans, she thought unhappily, holding her throbbing head.

Her drenching in the rain, combined with the shock she had received the previous afternoon, must have given her a chill which her swim this morning appeared to have turned into a raging cold. She felt unable to do anything but go back to bed again, where she soon began to feel even worse.

When, in the middle of the morning, Hilary found her she had tossed all her blankets off without actually realising what she was doing. The girl, after one apprehensive glance at her, hurried downstairs in alarm to tell Mrs Swinden. Mrs Swinden, after paying a grumbling visit to Helen's room, returned double-quick to ring Stein's secretary. A few minutes later, when she spoke to Stein, he told her to ring for a doctor immediately.

He surprised them by arriving at Oakfield before the doctor, which didn't appear to please him. He rang the doctor himself, to ask what was keeping him, and returned to Helen's bedside, violence in his stride as he regarded her flushed face and glazed eyes.

'Why didn't you say you were feeling ill?' he demanded, taking hold of her wrist and frowning at her racing pulse.

'I had a headache, that's all,' Helen murmured feebly. She wondered what Stein was doing here at this time of day. She couldn't see his face very well, it was floating above her in the most peculiar way, but she sensed he was frowning and he sounded annoyed.

'You should have mentioned it, all the same.'

Such terse, angry tones! Hadn't Hilary said his secretary had mentioned, when Mrs Swinden rang, that he was in the middle of an important conference with some of his directors? They must have told him she was dying and he had come for the pleasure of seeing her draw her last breath. Naturally he would be furious, now that he'd discovered she merely had a chill.

When she accused him of this, in a shrill, disjointed voice, he told her to be quiet. 'You're delirious, Helen. Don't say another word until you're able to talk sense!'

He prowled around her room so restlessly she wished he would sit down. When she grew tired of trying to keep up with him, she closed her eyes wearily.

She heard him opening the door, muttering savagely about there not being a bell in her room. She heard him shouting for Mrs Swinden to bring him something to drink. She couldn't remember hearing Stein raising his voice before and for several minutes her fevered mind pondered on this curiously.

She felt his fingers on her pulse again and wondered why he should be giving it so much attention. 'Have you had anything since that cup of tea we had before we went swimming?' he asked curtly.

She didn't answer, and he asked Mrs Swinden when she arrived with a laden tray. Helen was faintly surprised, since she had never seen Mrs Swinden carrying a tray before. When the housekeeper replied, somewhat primly, that Helen hadn't come down for breakfast but they had thought she was just having a lazy morning, he snapped something at the woman which Helen hoped vaguely wasn't what she thought it was, otherwise he might have made an enemy for life!

He asked Helen if she was thirsty. She was, but she feared if she tried to swallow anything she might be sick. She tried to explain this to him, but he either mustn't have listened or understood. The next thing she knew he was slipping an arm under her shoulders in order to lift her and press a little brandy to her dry lips.

Again his face floated, grey and strangely tense above her, and she had a sudden desire to cling to him for comfort. 'Stein ...' she whispered, turning her pale head against his shoulder instead of towards the drink he held.

'You'd better have something, Helen,' she heard him draw a harsh breath while his body went rigid. 'Just a little sip of this might help. I've added a lot of water.'

She was relieved when the doctor came, because Stein refused to leave her alone. She felt too ill to appreciate his frequent attempts to bathe her brow and tidy her bed. Fretfully she appealed to Mrs Swinden that she didn't want to be washed and made to drink and have her bed made, but when Mrs Swinden, for once surprisingly sympathetic, spoke up in support of her, Stein practically ordered her out of the room.

Helen was glad when the doctor ordered Stein out too, although he went grimly and with obvious reluctance.

The doctor, who had known Helen since she was a baby, muttered fussily as he examined her. 'I don't suppose anyone's ever told Mr Maddison what to do in his life, at least not for years. He certainly seems to take his responsibilities seriously. Your father couldn't have left you in better hands.'

Doctor Palmer was right in some ways, Helen reflected bitterly, if not in others. Stein did take her seriously, but she wasn't exactly his responsibility, and she was grateful that her father had made no attempt to put such a request in his will. He had left Stein a few personal belongings—his gun and some pictures he had prized—but hadn't asked him to take care of Helen. If Stein had a position in her life it was self-appointed. He was concerned for her well-being only because he was determined she wouldn't cheat him of his revenge.

The doctor diagnosed a severe chill and kept Helen in bed for the next week. She was so ill he was frightened

of complications, but fortunately she escaped anything
more serious. This might have been due to the
competence of the private nurse Stein engaged. Helen
couldn't understand why he went to so much trouble,
especially when she was sure she didn't need any special
treatment and Mrs Swinden said she was more than
willing to look after her.

The nurse was a pleasant girl and Helen liked her.
When the time came she was really sorry to see her go.

'I'm very grateful for all you've done for me,' Helen
said sincerely, as she shook the girl's hand, 'but I still
feel an awful fraud. There must have been a lot of
people who needed you much more than I did.'

'People need nurses all the time, fortunately—or
unfortunately,' the nurse smiled humorously, 'but you
were very ill, dear. If I hadn't been here you might have
had to go into hospital. However, Mr Maddison didn't
let it come to that.'

'No,' Helen murmured, well aware of Jane Smith's
curiosity regarding Stein. She came from London and
had apparently heard of him before she had arrived.
She appeared slightly in awe of his reputation as one of
the City's leading tycoons, and Helen wondered if she
had fallen in love with him, as she usually flushed
whenever he'd entered her room.

He had come to her room so frequently that Helen
had begun to suspect he might return the nurse's
feelings. Stein liked women and seemed to prefer those
nearer his own age. Jane Smith's uncle was a famous
Harley Street consultant and the girl was very pretty
and intelligent. As a possible candidate for the position
of his wife—if Stein should ever decide to get married—
Jane Smith might be eminently suitable.

CHAPTER SEVEN

THE HOUSE seemed very quiet after Jane Smith had gone. She left with Stein, and it gave Helen little pleasure to see them sitting together in the back of the Rolls. As she gazed at them from behind the drawing-room curtains, to where she had furtively sped to watch them depart, she saw that Stein appeared to be giving the girl all his attention. Unhappily Helen frowned, thinking she understood why he had insisted that Jane stayed an extra week.

Refusing to admit a bitter surge of jealousy, Helen wandered restlessly until lunch. Her illness had left her easily depressed and the as yet unsolved problem of her future didn't help. A little winter sunshine crept through the windows but it wasn't bright enough to cheer her up.

Her thoughts kept returning to Stein and Jane. Undoubtedly Stein was a brilliant tactician. Helen didn't know why she hadn't realised this until now. He had kept the nurse here as much for his own benefit as Helen's. She must have helped to enliven a few very dull winter evenings.

Angrily Helen wondered what all the care he had lavished on her during the past days really amounted to. He probably considered it was his fault she had been so ill, as he had made her go swimming. He must have believed he owed her something, because, during the worst nights of her illness, whenever she had opened her eyes he had been there. And once, when she had admittedly been burning up and delirious, she had thought she had heard him quarrelling with the nurse over her. The next morning, when she had been lucid again and asked about it, Jane had muttered crossly

113

something about Mr Maddison being extremely high-handed and trying to teach her her own business.

It was comforting to know someone else realised he had his faults, Helen thought bitterly, without stopping to consider whether she was being fair or not. He might have been justified in accusing her of throwing her weight about, but she hoped she never did it quite so indiscriminately!

Perhaps, she brooded, she should have done more to encourage his friendship with Jane. Helen was annoyed with herself for not having thought of this sooner. She might have saved herself the trouble of struggling to join them these last few evenings for dinner. She didn't ask herself why she had, especially when, to begin with anyway, the effort had nearly been too much for her. It wasn't as if she had contributed a great deal to the conversation either. Usually she had sat in a daze of weariness and must have looked as though she was about to pass out any minute. Which, unfortunately, had kept Stein's eyes on her instead of Jane, as he obviously hadn't been prepared for the embarrassment of having her fainting all over his dinner table!

Ignoring how the thought of them dining alone had been unendurable, Helen now decided she had been very foolish. If Stein had a fiancée or wife he would have to let her go! No other woman would tolerate her living here alone with him. Somehow she had to convince him he would be better off married and concentrating on a wife and family instead of herself. She couldn't understand why such a brilliant idea should make her feel almost ill again.

In fact she felt so miserable and desperately lonely that when a friend rang just before lunch, asking her to tea, she accepted gratefully.

'I heard you were getting better,' Beryl said eagerly, 'and you did promise when I saw you in the village, remember? I'm simply dying to hear all your news!'

Helen did remember. It was the day she and Stein

had quarrelled over the trees Charlie Parkinson had been cutting down. She had met Beryl in the village that afternoon and promised to call. The Phillips were neighbours, and if they had never been close friends, she and Beryl had met frequently at local events.

She accepted Beryl's invitation with something akin to relief. She had been going out daily for a walk with Jane and she missed her cheerful company. The rest of the day didn't seem to stretch so endlessly, now she had something to look forward to.

Beryl promised she would send her brother to pick Helen up as she had no transport and Helen told Mrs Swinden where she was going as she went to get ready. Mrs Swinden might not have turned over a completely new leaf, but since Helen had been ill she had treated her with much more respect. Helen wasn't sure if respect was quite the right word, but she didn't feel up to trying to discover whether Mrs Swinden's new attitude was genuine or not.

Gary Phillips arrived promptly at three-thirty and drove Helen straight to his home. It had been over four years since she had seen him, as he had been abroad. She smiled as she ran to meet him on the drive, to save him the bother of getting out of his car, and he whistled when he saw her.

'Who'd have thought it?' he exclaimed with a laugh, out of the car in a flash, as good manners and the extremely attractive picture Helen made prompted him to exert himself. 'The last time we met I think you had pigtails and a brace on your teeth.'

'I was still at school,' she admitted the pigtails but not the brace. 'That must have been someone else.'

He grinned. 'Now you're a beautiful woman.'

'I'm twenty-one,' she acknowledged that much. 'Almost.'

'A great age,' he laughed, tucking her in carefully.

She liked Gary. He drove a low, racy sports model and was fun. She discovered he was very easy to talk to and didn't disturb her the way Stein did. He must be about thirty, she thought, for he was older than Beryl, and she didn't think he was married.

High Towers, his home, was definitely a showplace. Helen hadn't been there for a long time, but it didn't seem to have changed. Mr and Mrs Phillips were out but Beryl said her mother would be in later and hoped Helen would stay to dinner.

Helen hesitated, then shook her head. She didn't refuse because of Stein, as she believed he might be staying in town this evening. She had thought, these last few days, that her lack of interest had annoyed him, but for her own sake she had tried to put some distance between them. One day he would get tired of baiting her and throw her out, and she was becoming increasingly certain that if she escaped with nothing worse than a few bruises she might be lucky. Bruises would fade, but she knew of no cure for a broken heart.

'I don't think I have enough energy yet,' she replied ruefully to Beryl, 'and I'd have to go home again and change. Another time, perhaps.'

Beryl nodded and began making a great fuss of her. She made her sit close beside the warm fire and rang immediately for tea. 'How is Stein?' she asked, pouring Helen a cup and passing a plate of biscuits. 'I haven't seen him for a while.'

Gary, lounging in a chair by Helen's side, laughed sarcastically. 'She's been waiting all day to ask.'

Beryl, shooting him a withering glance, said sharply, 'Don't take any notice of him, Helen. Stein's taken me out a few times, and I consider we're friendly enough for me to ask how he's keeping.'

Helen felt herself go suddenly pale and hoped the other two didn't notice. So Beryl was another of Stein's conquests. She wondered how many more she would meet. 'As far as one can tell he's keeping very well,' she answered carefully.

'What does he do in London every day?' Beryl

enquired eagerly, and, when Helen didn't reply, 'Why do you think he's never married? I mean, with his looks and money, you'd think someone would have grabbed him long ago.'

'Don't imagine a lot of women haven't tried,' Gary drawled cynically while Helen winced at Beryl's outspokenness. 'I knew him in New York, before he came to settle in this neck of the woods.'

Helen realised she had no idea exactly what Stein had done or where he had lived before she had known him. She had naturally assumed he had lived in London, but with business connections all over the world, it could have been any city, anywhere.

Beryl didn't seem too disappointed by Helen's inability to satisfy her curiosity, but Helen soon became aware that it might only be a matter of time before Beryl began asking more pertinent questions. She tried to divert her without success, and was dismayed but not surprised when her worst fears were realised.

'Tell me, darling,' said Beryl, with a concern which Helen couldn't believe was genuine, 'now that you don't have your father any more, can you go on living with Stein at Oakfield? I don't know what your exact position is, of course, but everyone's wondering. I know you'll forgive me, but as an old friend . . .'

Fortunately, at this point the doorbell rang, resounding through the house, interrupting Beryl's sugar-sweet discourse. Whoever was there was obviously full of impatience.

Beryl paused with a frown, her attention now riveted on what appeared to be a minor commotion in the hall, but even as her hand stretched towards the bell, presumably with the intention of finding out what was going on, the door burst open and Stein strode in. A servant hovered behind him, but he shut the door in the man's face.

He didn't seem in a good mood. Helen stared at him, feeling cold and sick with alarm. He looked positively livid, and she shrank from him involuntarily.

Approaching her, he ignored both Beryl and Gary as he jerked her ruthlessly to her feet. 'Why did you come here?' he asked curtly. 'You know you aren't fit to be out!'

Trembling a little with surprise and fright, Helen swallowed. Stein's mouth was a taut line and she felt frozen by his icy stare.

'I felt like a change,' she explained.

He said coldly. 'You should have waited until you were stronger.'

Beryl, regaining her customary composure, came pouting to his side. The startled expression on her face was replaced by one of triumph. 'It's nice of you to call, Stein,' she smiled. 'I haven't seen you for ages. Couldn't you stay for dinner? Helen won't, but Gary could take her home.'

He merely glanced at her and refused politely before turning his attention to Helen again. 'Where's your coat?' he asked curtly.

'I didn't bring one.'

He looked ready to explode, and Helen shivered at the burning rage in his eyes. 'You must be out of your mind!' he snapped.

She stared at him, clenching her hands in an effort to stop herself trembling. 'I thought I'd be warm enough in Gary's car.'

'You need your head examined!'

'There's no need to bully her!' Gary intervened for the first time. 'She didn't come to any harm.'

'That remains to be seen.' Stein stared at him contemptuously.

Helen felt the hot colour rise to her cheeks. The last thing she wanted was to quarrel with Stein in front of Beryl and Gary. Stein wasn't considering her at all. He seemed bent on humiliating her. She could see the antagonism in Beryl's eyes as he calmly disposed of her clinging arm, and the sharpness in Gary's. She had no wish to be the subject of their idle curiosity, once she and Stein had gone. Didn't he realise how they might speculate? They weren't good enough friends to believe the situation between Stein and herself was none of their business.

'You aren't by any chance accusing me of anything?' she heard Gary asking Stein belligerently.

Stein stared at him coldly. 'I'm very familiar with what goes on in New York.'

Gary appeared to lose some of his boldness and colour. 'Everyone sows a few wild oats, even you,' he retorted.

'I wasn't aware we were making comparisons,' Stein snapped. 'Where would you like to begin?'

Immediately Gary backed down. Helen wondered why. Gary's rather chubby good looks didn't exactly suggest vice of any kind. She would have thought Stein's love affairs might be much more lurid than anything Gary had indulged in.

'I'm sure the girls have no wish to be bored,' Gary muttered.

'Bored isn't perhaps the word I would have chosen,' Stein returned cynically.

Gary gasped, retreating from such cool derision in a way which made Helen suspect her snap judgment of his character had been inaccurate. Stein obviously knew things about him that he had no wish to be made public. Glancing at the cold mockery in Stein's face, Helen thought she could understand Gary's apprehension. Stein would make a very good friend but a terrible enemy!

She was so disturbed she swayed, going very white. Instantly aware of this, Stein put his arm firmly around her, while Beryl stared at her with sullen, accusing eyes.

Shifting uncomfortably, Gary cleared his throat. 'You don't have to take her home, Mr Maddison,' he said truculently, with the air of a man determined to make one last stand, even if the odds were stacked against him. 'I brought Helen here and I'd like to take her back.'

'There's no point, now I'm here,' Stein snapped. 'Helen comes with me.'

Clearly intent on carrying out his threat, he turned to leave, but Helen, although she trembled, resisted stubbornly. 'Don't I have any say in the matter, Stein?'

'Are you determined to make a scene?'

Helen heard the underlying menace in his voice and was aware of his hand firmly on her waist, and of the tremors it was sending through her. Beryl's eyes were fixed on it and her mouth had a vicious little twist which Helen remembered from the past. Beryl might be fun, but she could also be extremely unpleasant when something displeased her.

The flush on Helen's face deepened. 'I would like to stay a little longer . . .'

'No,' Stein put his foot down uncompromisingly, his fingers digging in her flesh warning her to give in.

'I—I haven't been here much more than an hour.' She still tried to fight him, although she realised that later he might easily make her suffer for it.

'You've been ill,' Stein's mouth tightened. 'You shouldn't have been out at all on a night like this. Now come on!'

She turned her head to look at him, again meeting a wholly ruthless expression. Instinctively she sensed she didn't have that much time. If she persisted in arguing he was going to say or do something which might make her regret she hadn't obeyed him immediately.

What Beryl and Gary were thinking she couldn't imagine! Stein had practically forced his way in and hadn't even tried to be tactful. Knowing Beryl's spite and the length of her tongue, Helen suspected that everything that had happened since Stein arrived would be quickly relayed to as many of her friends in the district as would be prepared to listen. And a lot would, she thought bitterly. Not so much happened in these parts, in the depth of winter, that people could afford to pass up a juicy morsel of gossip like this.

Helen had a wild desire to round on Stein angrily and tell him what he could do with all his apparent care and attention. Yet suddenly, when she was about to, her courage failed her. She would tell him what she thought of him, but later. Suddenly, surprisingly, all she wanted to do was go home. Anywhere where she could be alone, away from Beryl and Gary's prying glances and Stein's disapproving stare.

Shivering and weary, she knew she had to get away. Forcing a smile to her lips, she said a quick goodbye. 'Stein's probably right,' she admitted, in a last attempt to make everything seem normal. 'I have been ill and caused a lot of bother. And I think he feels responsible for me because of my father.'

As they drove back to Oakfield, Stein said savagely, 'You could make a living as an actress one day. After I'm finished with you!'

'Will I have to work?' she mumbled, in a haze of tiredness.

'How do you mean?' he frowned.

She scarcely knew what she was saying, or why she should choose that particular moment to provoke him. 'After a man is finished with a woman, doesn't he usually provide her with ample compensation?'

'You've had that already,' he snapped. 'I'm the one who hasn't received anything!'

He would never forgive or trust her again, she realised, her eyes suddenly heavy with pain. All his actions were laced with violence, while he was continually suspicious of everything she did or said. She could feel in him the perpetual need to punish. Not once when he held her had he displayed any tenderness, only a driving desire to make her suffer.

She didn't reply, saving her energy, with a kind of growing hopelessness for the confrontation which would undoubtedly come. She didn't have much

strength left; Stein's anger appeared to have drained
her of it almost completely.

In the study, which she was gradually training herself
to think of as his, she asked suddenly, 'Who told you
where I was? Mrs Swinden?'

He thrust her none too gently into the same chair
where she had sat on the dreadful afternoon her father's
will had been read and he had found her running down
the drive. Her heart was beating over fast and she
refused to believe it was because he had insisted on
carrying her from the car. She could still feel his strong
arms around her, his breath on her face as he had
stared at her grimly and silently.

When she mentioned Mrs Swinden he paused as he
straightened. 'I told her to get in touch with me if ever
you attempted to leave Oakfield.'

'I was only with friends!'

His mouth tightened, but he didn't comment.

'I suppose you asked where I was as soon as you
returned from London?' Helen said sharply.

Stein bent over her, his eyes hard and glittering,
allowing her to feel the full force of his anger. 'I was in
my office when she rang,' he said bitingly.

'Your office!' Helen's face went an angry red, her
voice incredulous. 'You mean you actually asked her to
spy on me?'

He was entirely unmoved by her flare of temper. 'I
have to have someone keeping an eye on you.'

'To think,' Helen raged, 'I was beginning to trust
her!'

'Since I pay her,' Stein grated, 'she has to do as I say.
I wouldn't be too hard on her.'

Helen began grappling with the implications of what
she had just learnt. She stared at him, her chin tilted,
her blue eyes angry but bewildered. 'When Mrs
Swinden rang you must have dropped everything and
come straight home?'

'A brilliant piece of deduction!' Suddenly he reached

out, drawing her to her feet again, his hands gripping her savagely, as if she continued to madden him. 'But in future you'll stay here, unless you're going somewhere with me. I won't have you going out with anyone else.'

Trembling, she muttered, 'You don't own me!'

His face was masklike and hard. 'I've told you I want you. Men like Gary Phillips can wait their turn.'

She flushed at the contempt in his voice. 'I don't know how you feel able even to touch me,' she whispered, 'since your opinion of me is so low. I think you're crazy!'

'Your thoughts don't interest me,' he replied witheringly and with emphasis.

'I know they don't,' she retorted with a little more spirit. 'You demonstrated that quite clearly in front of the Phillips. What do you imagine people are going to say when they hear about what happened today? You could have been more tactful. As it is, the whole countryside is talking.'

His mouth quirked cynically. 'I don't have to ask where you got that information from.'

'Beryl wouldn't lie to me.'

His hands tightened contemptuously on her arms. 'She sounds a fine friend!'

'She probably considered it her duty to tell me.' Helen tried to free herself from his painful grip, but he wouldn't let her go. 'Isn't that what friends are for?'

'I wouldn't have thought so. I'd advise you not to see her again.'

'Yet you take her out,' she exclaimed.

The grey eyes held a chilling anger. 'I'm afraid you're mistaken. I've met her on one or two social occasions locally, but that's all.'

A flutter of relief touched Helen's heart like a balm and she closed her eyes briefly so Stein wouldn't see it. When she looked at him again her face was expressionless.

'We aren't just arguing about the Phillips, though,

are we? You're trying to keep me a prisoner. You don't want me going out and mixing with anybody, least of all my old friends.'

Stein studied her without relaxing an inch. 'Not until you're stronger and I'm able to come with you.'

'I am stronger,' she insisted defiantly, 'and if you don't let me go my reputation will soon be in shreds!'

His eyes smouldered derisively. 'It's been in that state for a while, I imagine, and nobody's fault but your own.'

The tension in him was so strong it made her quiver, but she felt too weary to try convincing him afresh how wrong he was about her. He wouldn't believe her, anyway. 'Your attitude isn't helping,' she said dully.

'I won't let you go,' he snapped.

His face was taut, and Helen shrank from such cold determination. Her heart was beating too rapidly as her temper rose again. 'Why don't you keep me locked up somewhere out of sight?' she cried. 'You won't let me go, but I believe you're secretly ashamed of me. Perhaps my so-called reputation is more than you can bear!'

'It could be,' he muttered harshly, an odd hoarseness in his voice.

If his admission startled her, she didn't know what to make of it. 'Why not think again, then?' she suggested hopefully.

He laughed without humour, staring down at her. 'All I can think of, night and day, is this,' he said thickly, his hands beginning slowly to move up her arms.

As Helen stood as though hypnotised, his fingers trailed over her shoulders to draw her closer. With his head bending towards her, his intention clear to read in the smouldering darkness of his eyes, she began trembling, but was unable to stir. One part of her felt starved for his kisses, while she wanted to run from the raging frustration she sensed in him. Yet she dared not even struggle. Suddenly she had no desire to incite further violence and would have given anything to have been able to soothe him.

She knew there must be a way, but inspiration failed her, defeated in the end by her traitorous senses which destroyed her ability to think. Would it always be like this? she wondered, as his lips paused a mere fraction from her own.

She started in alarm as he caught her long hair in a cruel grip. Suddenly realising the danger of the situation, she tried to struggle free of him. Expecting some form of brutal retaliation because of this, she was surprised when his mouth merely touched hers lightly before moving to her neck. He was treating her with a restraint which puzzled her as she could feel a threatening tenseness in his long, lean body.

'Don't fight me,' he whispered, inadvertently confirming her suspicions, 'or I won't guarantee not to hurt you.'

Helplessly she closed her eyes. What was the use of fighting? She might have been able to defend herself against one, but not two! Her own emotions were proving too treacherous for her. Every time Stein kissed her the feelings he aroused grew wilder, filling her with an increasing warmth and passion. Passion was something she had never experienced before and it frightened her a little, but if Stein was determined to keep her here what did anything else matter?

She heard the hard thud of his heart against her as his mouth closed over hers again. Blindly she clung to him, her arms going tightly around his neck, her fingers thrusting into the thick dark hair. The glitter in his eyes as he cupped her breasts made her draw a sharp, protesting breath, but she was too overwhelmed and dazed to protest.

He pulled her closer, his hands grasping her fiercely, then relaxing to wander restlessly over her. Her heart began beating as quickly as his and a yielding weakness turned her limbs to water. When he felt her resistance fading, the pressure of his mouth eased slightly, and she became aware of a more gentle exploration which was even more arousing than force.

'You know how much I want you,' he muttered thickly.

Helen's head was throbbing with a strange fever, her throat dry. She tried to speak, because his words seemed menacing, but she couldn't find her voice. And when she attempted to push him away, she couldn't find any strength. She thought she must be in some kind of trance as she just wanted to stay where she was and forget everything. In the dusky light Stein's face was poignantly familiar and her eyes went yearningly to his mouth, clearly betraying her inner hunger. A low moan escaped her, full of unconscious pleading as his words tormented her.

'I want to hear you say it,' he muttered hoarsely. 'You have to beg!'

Had she betrayed herself so unashamedly? Humiliation drowned the hot tide of passion in her veins. 'I can't!' she whispered huskily.

'Why not?' his voice was harsh. 'It can only be words you're afraid of.'

What he implied was obvious, but she still couldn't tell him she was innocent. 'I don't feel so good,' she murmured bleakly.

She heard him breathing roughly, as though he sought to regain a slipping control. There was a chilling fury in his eyes and a savage twist to his lips. 'You won't have that excuse much longer,' he snapped. 'My patience is rapidly coming to an end. I don't give a damn whether you hate me or not, but at least I can stop you thinking of other men.'

'I'm ill,' she insisted, the chill in his voice making her feel she actually was, and forcing her to cling to any form of protection.

'You were,' he taunted. 'Now you're just using it as an excuse.'

Helen flushed with shame and a flicker of rebellion.

'Can you wonder that I'm confused?'

'No,' he grated, releasing her so abruptly she almost fell, 'but I think it's your own feelings causing the confusion, not mine. For years you've been the spoiled daughter of a wealthy business man. Now that both the man and his wealth have disappeared, you're like a ship without a rudder adrift on stormy seas.'

She closed her eyes like a frightened child against the blazing rage in his hard face. How could he be so cruel? Of course he was basing his assumptions on what he thought he knew of her—and that he would never be prepared to overlook.

'I'm sorry,' she whispered stiffly, fighting a desperate desire to confess everything and throw herself on his mercy. Dully she returned to their former argument, thinking it safer. 'You have to remember I've lived here most of my life and it hurt to hear how neighbours and friends are speculating over me.'

'Don't worry,' Stein said dryly, 'I have enough money and influence to put a stop to that whenever I feel like it.'

Helen sighed unhappily. She wondered if he knew what he was talking about. How could money restore a reputation? And it was her problem, not his.

'Go and get changed,' he continued coldly, as she stared at him silently. 'If you were feeling fit enough to go out for tea, I'll take you out to dinner. I can't have you complaining you never get anywhere.'

What would it be like sharing a probably intimate table in a restaurant with a man whose head was filled only with thoughts of reprisal? Her face paled as she decided it might be more than she could stand. Swaying on her feet, she asked, 'Could we make it tomorrow night instead?'

Stein's jaw tightened as he caught her, swinging her up again in his arms. 'Have you no sense?' he rasped at her, as he had done earlier. 'I can't have either,' he acknowledged angrily, not giving her a chance to protest as he carried her grimly to her room. 'We both know you aren't completely well yet. You can have your dinner in bed and we'll go out some other time.'

Stein spent the rest of the week working at home. He had his secretary brought from London and she stayed until the weekend. During the day she and Stein were closeted in the study, but Helen had dinner with them each evening. On Saturday morning, after Paul had departed with Mrs Wilkinson for London, Stein informed Helen that they would be going to town themselves, later, as he thought she was sufficiently recovered to enjoy the evening out they had postponed.

'You're looking much better,' he said, as they set out. 'You look charming, and I like your dress.'

He was driving himself with Helen sitting comfortably beside him, and she glanced up in surprise at his cordial tones. There was usually very little kindness in his voice when he spoke to her, although this week, when Mrs Wilkinson had been around, he had contrived to be reasonably pleasant.

'You've seen to it that I am better,' she replied coolly, resenting the way in which he had deliberately concentrated on improving her health over the past few days. Despite his heavy work load, he had taken time to ensure she had a good walk each afternoon, and, at dinner, he had insisted she ate everything on her plate. He had even sent Hilary to her room with hot milk after she had gone to bed. What Mrs Wilkinson thought of it she had no idea, but she suspected Stein's middle-aged secretary was curious. Everyone was curious, Helen thought despairingly; it wasn't only Beryl!

'I've done my best,' she heard Stein saying smoothly. 'After all, you wouldn't have been ill but for me.'

'I didn't think I was that much on your conscience,' she said dryly.

He shrugged. 'There are other reasons why I wanted you well again.'

Because she didn't want to dwell on the other reasons, Helen said sharply, 'Was it absolutely necessary to bring Mrs Wilkinson here? She doesn't miss much. I don't know what she must be thinking.'

'Do you spend all your days wondering what other people are thinking?' he asked acidly. 'It's a pity you didn't begin when you were younger!'

Helen clenched her hands tightly and he slanted her a quick glance before adding curtly, 'This isn't the first time I've taken a working break.'

'The study isn't very well suited for operations on your scale,' Helen retorted dubiously.

'I can work almost anywhere. So can my secretary,' said Stein.

'So,' she muttered flatly, 'it wasn't just to make sure I didn't run away.'

She was surprised at the dull flush over his hard cheekbones. 'Partly it was,' he admitted, 'but not altogether. I like Oakfield. It's the home I never had before.'

'I'm sure it's not because you couldn't afford one,' she retorted, hurt goading her as he made her realise Oakfield wouldn't be her home much longer.

'It's time I've always been short of, not money,' he replied as sharply.

'Gary mentioned that you'd lived in New York,' she suddenly remembered.

'On and off.' He glanced narrowly at her frowning face, then changed the subject slightly. 'Gary Phillips works for his uncle over there. The old man's a leading light in the city, but Gary isn't reputed to be so brilliant. Do you know him well?'

Helen decided to be honest. There seemed no point in being anything else. 'I haven't seen much of him for years. I must have been only a child when he went away, not old enough to attract his attention.'

'You are now, though.'

Despairingly she glanced at him. 'I didn't even know

he was home until the other day when Beryl said he would collect me.'

'And you haven't seen him since? He hasn't been around?'

'Not unless he's been hiding behind some bushes while I've been out for a walk?'

'I'd have heard,' Stein assured her coldly, 'if he'd been anywhere near. Somehow I don't think he will be again. He's not the sort to push his luck.'

Helen sighed, sensing from his flat, controlled tones it might be futile to argue. He drove smoothly and talked evenly, but she was nervously aware of his hidden anger. She had thought to take advantage of his slightly relaxed mood in order to plead to be allowed to look for a job, but noting the renewed grimness of his face she realised the hopelessness of making such a request. Stein hadn't changed. She'd be a fool to imagine, because of his more tolerant manner over the past few days, that he had! He must be as determined as ever to carry out his former threats.

She had borrowed money which she couldn't repay, among other things. Bleakly she turned her head, catching a certain expression in the cold grey eyes watching her. Apprehensively Helen's heart lurched while her lips went dry. What made her think he was planning something even worse than she had envisaged, something which might make his previous plans seem almost merciful by comparison?

CHAPTER EIGHT

SINCE she knew Stein's preference for smaller, more intimate places, Helen's brow pleated in a faintly puzzled frown as they entered the vestibule of the large London hotel and he guided her into the cocktail lounge for drinks before dinner. As they sat down at a small, round table she tried to disregard a renewed sensation of apprehension. She could see no one she knew, and even if there had been it wouldn't have mattered.

She became aware of Stein staring at her with slightly raised brows. 'Is there anything wrong?'

'No, why should there be?' She was instantly on the defensive.

His mouth thinned. 'You were looking worried.'

She wished he wouldn't keep remarking on every expression that crossed her face, because very few seemed to please him! Hastily she shook her head, making some attempt to smile. How could she explain she felt cold and alone? Stein would never understand. He would only be angry, and the evening might turn into a disaster before it had even begun!

'I'm sorry,' she murmured huskily, a soft flush on her cheeks as his continuing regard disturbed her. 'Perhaps it's because I haven't been out for a while.'

'Three weeks?'

'It seems longer.'

'I can agree with that!'

She glanced at him quickly. His voice was bitter, his face hard. A resigned sigh escaped her tremulous lips, but this time he didn't appear to notice. His attention was suddenly riveted on a woman approaching them.

The lady was elegant and pretty but clearly well into

131

middle age. Idly Helen wondered what it was about her
that had caught Stein's eye. She was startled to realise
he must know her as he rose to greet her when she
paused beside them. Helen was even more surprised
when the woman clasped him by the arms and he bent
to kiss her lightly on her cheek.

'Estella!' she heard him say gently. 'As lovely as ever!'

Helen thought she detected a faint mockery in
Estella's eyes as she smiled warmly. 'It's been a long
time, Stein.'

'Over a year,' his eyes teased as he turned the full
shaft of his charm on her. 'We mustn't let it be so long
again.'

'We always say that,' Estella laughed ruefully. 'The
other day, in Paris, when I began counting how long it
has been, I felt I had to come and see you. I'm only here
for the night, mind you, as Hank's been asking for days
when I'm coming home, but I hope it's convenient?'

'Actually,' Stein said smoothly, with a sideways
glance at Helen, 'you couldn't have come at a better
time. I wanted you to be the first to congratulate me
and meet my fiancée.'

Helen's breath caught in her throat and froze there.
Who did he say? She gazed at him in blind confusion as
he drew her to her feet. His grip was gentle, but the
message which flashed briefly through his eyes, for her
alone, was not. Play along, it commanded, or else!

There was nothing threatening in his face as he
introduced her to a very curious Estella, and his silent
warning might have been unnecessary as Helen was too
stunned to do more than react like a puppet.

'My stepmother,' he explained the beaming lady, who
enclosed Helen in a delightfully perfumed and sweeping
embrace, while Stein signalled to their waiter to bring
champagne.

'We must celebrate,' he said.

'Oh, yes!' Estella agreed, without appearing to notice
that Helen was speechless. 'I'm so pleased to meet you,

my dear,' she said to Helen. 'You must forgive me if I seem over-excited, but I'd no idea Stein was even thinking of getting married until today.'

Helen was about to say she hadn't known herself when she received another warning glance.

'It happened suddenly,' Stein explained.

'All the best things do!' Estella declared happily, as they sat down again.

Helen's lips stretched in what she presumed must have passed for a smile as Estella returned it. 'I can quite see how Stein fell for you,' she leant towards Helen and patted her hand approvingly. 'You're so pretty, and you've got a little extra something. I'm sure you and Stein will be very happy.'

Helen had never cared for people who talked incessantly, but for once she didn't mind. She soon gathered that Estella was married to an American she had met after Stein's father had died. She seemed to think it was essential to explain odd details to Helen.

'I haven't seen much of Stein since I married Hank, but we've always kept in touch. When he was in New York, of course, it was easier.'

'You aren't staying long in London?' Helen enquired, trying to avoid mentioning her so-called engagement. Although it made her terribly angry, she couldn't believe Stein intended her to take it seriously. Yet her mind revolted at this kind of joke and she didn't want to make a scene about it. Not until she got Stein alone!

'I'm just passing through,' Estella sighed. 'I was determined to look Stein up. I was happy I did when I rang him this morning and he told me his news. Now I'm dying to know when the wedding's going to be!'

'Not for a while,' Stein broke in. 'Helen's just lost her father, remember.'

'Oh, yes. How remiss of me!'

Stein must have told Estella quite a bit? Helen glanced at him sharply, wondering how much, as Estella touched her hand, this time sympathetically. 'He did mention it, and I'm sorry, honey, but knowing Stein's impatience I didn't think he would be prepared to wait.'

Helen smiled at her vaguely, taking another sip of champagne. She felt she really needed something stronger, but the sparkling wine was helping to take away all sense of reality.

'Where's your ring?' Estella exclaimed, after a brief pause, as though she was determined not to let anything cloud such a happy occasion. 'Oh, my, Stein, you've surely never forgotten the ring!'

Stein smiled, the grey eyes hard and brilliant, glittering with a force Helen could never withstand. To her dazed horror, he extracted a box from an inner pocket, opening it to reveal the glitter of diamonds.

'Oh, my!' Estella exclaimed again. 'That must be worth a fortune!'

'You should know.' As if to give Helen time to get over the shock, he glanced with dry affection over Estella's impressive array of jewellery.

'Hank's very good to me,' Estella smiled complacently. 'He likes spending money, and diamonds are a good investment.'

Helen's long lashes fluttered and her eyes looked glazed as Stein slid the ring on her slender white finger. She stiffened, wondering incredulously what he thought he was playing at. Marriage had no part, she was sure, in his devious schemes, and she failed to see either sense or reason in a phoney engagement.

Amazingly, as though the shock she was experiencing extended to every bit of her, her hand didn't tremble as Stein, carrying the charade further, lifted it to his mouth. Yet as soon as his lips touched her skin a sharp slither of fire rushed through her and her breathing quickened. The heat in her body bewildered her and she shivered faintly with fear.

She refused to look at Stein after he had dropped her hand back to her side. She had no desire to see the mockery which she knew would be in his eyes, or to allow him to see the apprehension which she was certain must lie at the back of her own.

Stein's stepmother was nice, too nice to deceive, Helen thought anxiously, hating Stein as Estella watched them almost tearfully. From the rather disjointed conversation, Helen realised her husband must be an oil man. Shades of Dallas, she decided wryly, as Estella made some fleeting reference to his offices in the city and the miles he commuted from their ranch each day.

Estella looked as if her husband might be extremely wealthy. Apart from her fabulous jewellery, the clothes she wore must have cost a small fortune and she was very well groomed. A lot of people might have said she was a pleasure to look at, as long as one didn't have to foot the bills!

Ruefully Helen glanced down at her own dress. It hadn't been cheap, but it was obviously not in the same class as Estella's. She looked up to find Stein watching her, and he wasn't smiling. His eyes gleamed coolly as they moved over her, assessing every inch of her, and she was suddenly conscious of the fragile material, the silvery threads which moulded the swelling contours of her slender body. His gaze lingered on the smooth white skin of her throat before sliding to rest on the deep cleft between her breasts. She felt the burning tide of his possession and her heart thudded.

Nervously her lashes flickered and she hastily averted her blue eyes to blindly study Estella again.

'You seem interested in me?' Estella teased, as a waiter brought Stein a note and he excused himself to speak to a couple he knew.

Helen flushed, not attempting to deny it. Under Estella's froth and flutter lay real kindness, and a more discerning character than was at first apparent. 'I'm sorry,' she apologised.

Estella dismissed her apology with a careless wave of

her hand. 'I'm flattered, honey, not insulted. I know I often look a bit ostentatious, but Hank likes spending money on me and he likes me to show it. It becomes a habit in time, and I enjoy pleasing him.'

'You enjoy your life in Texas?'

'Oh, yes!'

Estella spoke exuberantly, but somehow Helen fancied she detected a slight pathos. It made her aware that however much one had there might still be drawbacks.

'Stein never told me about you,' she confessed impulsively, 'and I can't think why he didn't. Meeting you here, this evening, was a complete surprise.'

Estella didn't appear put out, she merely smiled. 'Stein's brilliant in his own field, but I believe he tends to keep his personal relationships apart, even to the extent of shutting them out. I was only married to his father a year before he died and we got on very well. Since I married again I haven't seen a lot of him. To tell you the truth,' she sighed, 'if I didn't bother to keep in touch I don't think he would.'

Helen hesitated. 'You must know he took over my father's firm?'

'Yes,' with a flicker of a glance in Stein's direction, Estella became more guarded. 'I was in London about the time, and he did mention it.'

Helen frowned, remembering how little Stein had divulged about himself and the few odd scraps of information she had avidly pounced on and believed. 'Sometimes it's not quite fair to other people, making them guess all the way, I mean.'

Estella shrugged wryly. 'That's him! You don't have to try and convince me he didn't tell you very much. When his mother died—she died from pneumonia, you know, when Stein was in his early teens. She caught a chill and neglected it. Well, from that day on, his father, my first husband, said he just seemed to close up.'

'I think perhaps it was my father's fault Stein didn't

tell me much about himself.' Helen tried to be honest, while her mind groped with what she'd just learned.

'Ah!' Estella smiled coyly. 'So your father disapproved of Stein as a suitor, did he? Was it because you were so young?'

'It might have been.' That wasn't what Helen had meant at all, but as giving a true explanation was impossible she decided to let it pass. She had been foolish to say anything in the first place, so it was her own fault if Estella jumped to the wrong conclusions.

'It must have been!' Estella was very emphatic. 'No man in his right mind would turn Stein Maddison down as a son-in-law.'

When Helen frowned unhappily, she laughed. 'You mustn't mind me, dear, I'm not very tactful, but you'll soon get used to me. And you have to admit Stein has a lot going for him.'

'Yes,' Helen whispered, unable to deny it.

Estella patted her hand, which Helen was coming to recognise as a mark of approval. 'He told me you'd been ill and I could tell he'd been worried. So much that I'm not surprised he loves you.'

Helen went quite cold. Whatever Stein's reasons for being worried, love didn't come into it. 'He was very kind,' she felt compelled to admit. 'He saw to it that I had a nurse and everything.'

'He would do,' Estella agreed. 'He's very thoughful. I'm glad he's found a girl like you, dear. A man in his position is very vulnerable, you know. I've prayed he wouldn't fall for someone out to marry him for his position and money.'

'I don't think he would allow that,' Helen muttered stiffly, wondering desperately what Estella would say if she knew how much money she owed Stein. Money she had little hope of paying back. Where was Stein? She glanced around feverishly, her long, thick hair swinging over her shoulders. He was talking to a couple a short distance away, and she wished he would hurry up and come back. Hadn't he any compunction about leaving her with his stepmother, who he must realise would talk of nothing but their phoney engagement!

A man paused by their table, scrutinising Helen's face intently. He was tall, youngish-looking, his face vaguely familiar.

'Forgive me,' he said, 'but it is Helen, isn't it? Helen Davis?'

'Donald Blyth!' Now that Helen remembered who he was, she was no less surprised. He worked for a leading international newspaper, often on assignments overseas. She had met him through her father, who had known and liked him. Helen had gone out with him once or twice but, like Gary Phillips, she hadn't seen anything of him for years. Because of his occupation he was the last man she would have wanted to see this evening! Swiftly, half instinctively, she clasped her hands together, to hide her ring.

'I thought it was you,' Donald was saying, smiling broadly. 'I wasn't sure, though, until you looked around. You're more beautiful than ever, Helen,' he added huskily. 'I always knew you'd turn into a beautiful woman!'

Helen was annoyed when she flushed. Aware of Estella watching with interest, she reluctantly introduced them.

'You're over from the States?' Donald bowed over Estella's hand with an old-world courtesy which Helen could see pleased her.

'This is a very special occasion!' Estella beamed. 'You won't know yet about Helen's engagement?'

Donald's eyes sharpened with disappointment and curiosity. 'I had no idea. I'm not always too late.'

As his eyes met hers, Helen knew what he was referring to. Uneasily she swallowed. Donald had become too attentive, too soon, and she hadn't felt a thing for him. They'd had a pretty explosive row—the explosion mostly on Donald's side. He had impressive family connections, as well as having proved himself in a profession where many failed. He had believed he was irresistible to most women and that a rather naïve girl, barely eighteen years old, should be a walk-over.

'Who's the lucky man?' he asked lightly, while his eyes went hard and amazingly angry, considering how long it was since he and Helen had met.

'It's not public yet,' she faltered evasively, silently but fervently willing him to lose interest and leave.

'It just happened this evening,' Estella revealed enthusiastically, obviously enjoying herself. She either ignored or didn't see the frantic warning in the slight shake of Helen's head. 'Helen has just got engaged to my stepson, Stein Maddison. Do you know him, Mr Blyth?'

'Know him?' Donald visibly paled. 'Who doesn't!'

At that moment Stein returned. He glanced at Donald as if he was something that had crawled out from under a stone. 'Hello, Blyth,' he nodded curtly, 'Still at it, are you?'

Donald returned his glance as grimly. 'I was just about to offer my congratulations.'

Stein, with one look at Estella's happy face and Helen's dismayed one, didn't need to be told what had happened. 'I won't have you pestering my fiancée, Blyth,' he said harshly.

'What makes you think she would object?' Donald asked silkily, obviously disliking Stein's manner. 'I've known Helen a long time, perhaps longer than you.'

'But not as well.'

'Stein,' Estella intervened hastily, 'as Mr Blyth is a friend of Helen's, why don't we ask him to join us? At least for a drink.'

Both men, eyeing each other coldly, seemed to dislike the idea. At last Donald said, 'Some other time, Mrs Rutherman, if you don't mind. I'm afraid I have an appointment and I'm late already.'

'How odd,' Estella complained, as with a last grim

stare at Helen, he turned and left them. 'Oh, I am sorry, honey,' she exclaimed. 'You did say he was an old friend.'

'Not that old.' Helen tried to speak lightly.

Stein was unconvinced by her careless tones. His eyes smouldered as they sat down to dinner. 'Blyth's one of the biggest hounds in Fleet Street. Once on the scent he never gives up.'

Estella laughed. 'He's not supposed to, darling. And anyway, you couldn't keep your engagement a secret. You didn't want to, did you?' She appeared rather disconcerted.

'No, of course not.' Stein was still staring at Helen and she sensed his anger. 'But men like Blyth aren't to be encouraged. They aren't easy to get rid of.'

Not as easy as Gary Phillips, Helen thought bitterly, remembering how Stein had ruthlessly cut him out of her life. Twice this week Gary had phoned and each time Stein had said she wasn't available. She wondered why Donald appeared to be worrying him. No doubt he would get the same kind of treatment if he tried to approach her. Stein gave little away, but she was sure he couldn't accuse her of deliberately provoking him this time. It wasn't her fault that Donald had given the impression of being a closer friend than he had been!

They went up to Estella's suite for coffee after they had eaten. Estella was expecting a call from her husband, and they just reached her suite as it came through. She excused herself to take it in her bedroom, leaving Helen and Stein alone.

The door had scarcely closed behind her when he rounded on Helen swiftly. 'Might I have fair warning,' he asked savagely, 'how many more men from your past I'm liable to meet?'

She backed away from the blackness of his eyes. 'S-so far you've only met two . . .'

'You realise Blyth's reputation with women?'

'That's not what I want to talk about,' she cried, with

a quick glance at the door through which Estella had disappeared. 'What about this,' she couldn't bear to say 'our', 'engagement?'

His lips curled. 'That can wait. When did you last see Blyth?'

'I—I can't remember . . .'

'Force yourself!'

She retreated again from his angry, possessive gaze, shaking her head, beginning to tremble. She came up against something hard and he caught her, advancing step by step until he suddenly swooped to grasp her bare shoulders.

'I should have asked how well you knew him!' he snapped, his hands hurting her.

Helen gasped at the cruelty in his face. 'I didn't,' she whispered.

His face was pale, his eyes blazing. 'You little bitch!' he snarled. 'I don't believe you, and I'll kill you if I hear of you even attempting to see him.'

'He hasn't asked me!'

She was shaking and shivering as though she had a fever, but he didn't appear to notice. The cold control he had exercised during dinner had gone. She could feel his heart thundering, although they were only lightly touching.

'No doubt he will!' Stein's voice rasped. 'If he doesn't want to break it, our engagement could be just the news he's looking for. There hasn't been much excitement in that line lately, and I don't want you granting him privileges on the strength of his being an old friend!'

Her blue eyes widened incredulously, searching his distorted features. 'I told you, I hardly know him!'

'You said the same about Gary Phillips,' he snapped contemptuously, 'but I've got eyes in my head. I've seen the way they both look at you.'

She flushed. 'They're men, aren't they?'

'You can certainly make them believe it!'

Helen stared at him as he drew a rough breath. She found it impossible to argue. Whatever she said Stein had an answer. 'Donald Blyth might be married now,' she protested futilely.

'He isn't,' Stein replied curtly. 'I had lunch with his father a couple of weeks ago. The family's rolling and they all have their share. I suppose that attracts you?'

Helen despairingly shook her head. She remembered Donald's family was wealthy. Suddenly it crossed her mind that if Donald was still fond of her he might be willing to lend her enough to repay Stein, to get her out of his clutches. It wasn't just money, but at least if she could give him that back it might stop her from feeling like a thief.

Stein, as always, was one jump ahead. 'There's going to be no easy way out, Helen.'

Helen's lashes swept across her cheeks so he wouldn't see her tears of frustration. 'I have to keep trying, which doesn't mean I'm going to cheat! It's you who's done that, by tricking me into a false engagement!'

His eyes blazed as he pulled her swiftly closer. 'You're mine and you'll stay mine until I'm ready to let you go. Which won't be until all your debts are settled—and I'm not just talking of money!'

Lifting her face, she stared at him dumbly, her lips quivering with the effort to speak, but she couldn't. Stein's eyes narrowed, penetrating the blueness of hers. Then, as the innocence he saw there obviously angered him, his glance slid savagely to her mouth. He looked as if he could cheerfully have stangled her. There was violence in the set of his head and shoulders and in his gaze as it grazed her white throat.

Suddenly, as if seeking an outlet for emotions no longer possible to suppress, his mouth was bruising hers, his kisses hungry and brutal. He crushed her to him until the buttons of his jacket began bruising her breasts. His mouth hurt, while the heated movements of his hands over her body threatened and cajoled at the same time. Helen gasped as her body yielded to the pressure he imposed on it, and she was shaking from the frightening tension she felt in him. When he released her abruptly with a smothered curse, she felt almost faint with relief.

'Is this your idea of how to treat a fiancée?' she choked.

'How I treat tramps!' he jeered coldly, watching her with a glint of satisfaction at the lingering fear in her face. 'And I'm not finished with you yet. When we get home I want to know all about you.'

'You already know everything,' she whispered.

'No, I don't!' he rapped. 'I'm discovering more each day, and I won't put up with further surprises. I want a list of all the men you knew—exactly how many!'

She shrank from the leashed fury in his voice. 'What if I can't remember?' she defied him unwisely, too shattered to think of a reply which might have calmed him down.

'You will!' he grated.

She gazed at him, her hands clammy. She had been out with plenty of men after Stein had entered her life, but she couldn't recall the names of half of them as they had been mostly senseless reprisal dates, meaning nothing. She had scarcely allowed any of them to touch her. There had only been the last one, from whom Stein had rescued her, but surely he didn't think they had all been like that? She squirmed with shame as she remembered that shameful incident.

Stein had known nothing serious had happened, and, although she knew he hadn't liked it, he had continued to treat her gently. What wouldn't she give for one of his tolerant smiles and a little gentleness now? Now it had all gone, and he looked at her with venom, not kindness!

Estella, returning to the sitting-room, smiled mischievously when she saw them standing close together. If she noticed the darkness of Stein's face, she probably put it down to frustration. They had coffee with her and she and Stein talked until well after midnight. Helen sat listening quietly, occasionally joining in, but not often. Most of the time she was desperately trying to think of a way out of the dilemma she was in.

'Don't forget,' said Estella, as they left her, 'I want an invitation to the wedding! In fact,' she addressed Helen, 'I'd love to come back and organise it for you. It would be nice for both of us as you have no parents and I haven't a daughter.'

In the car travelling back to Oakfield, Helen twisted the ring on her finger nervously. Estella appeared to like her and, if the circumstances had been different, they might have developed a pleasant relationship. There was anguish in her heart as she considered what might have been. If she hadn't been so blind she might have been married to Stein a year ago. Glancing at his hard profile, it came like a blow to realise she loved him. Once or twice before she had suspected it but managed to thrust such a possibility from her. Unhappily she found she could ignore it no longer, and the pain of it was almost unendurable. Stein must never guess—he would merely use it as another weapon against her. Her love for him might not be too difficult to hide if she was careful. But she could by no means be sure, with this new, overwhelming emotion flooding her, that she wouldn't somehow betray herself.

Stein slanted an impatient glance at her. 'Will you stop fiddling with your ring!' he snapped.

She had thought he was concentrating on his driving. 'It feels more like a ball and chain!' she muttered.

He didn't miss the slight quiver running through her. 'It's meant to be,' he retorted curtly. 'And a warning.'

'A warning?'

'To others. Do you think I have time to stand over you indefinitely?'

Her eyes widened at such deviousness. 'So that's why you dreamt up this bogus engagement? You don't trust me?'

'Not out of my sight, lady!'

She winced at the coldness of his voice. He must hate her a lot, and his opinion of her must be very low indeed to have forced him to go to such lengths. After Gary Phillips had shown he liked her, Stein must have thought she might appeal to Gary for help. He had been quick to realise that Gary, like most men, wouldn't be keen to assist a girl to betray her fiancé. Stein had it all worked out. He was a devil, Helen decided bitterly, always one step ahead. Introducing her to his stepmother this evening was another brilliant stroke. He might even come to consider her unexpected meeting with Donald Blyth an advantage too. Their engagement must now be virtually public knowledge and she couldn't break it and continue living at Oakfield. And at Oakfield she had no chance of escaping, not while she still owed Stein so much, both morally and financially.

He didn't trust her, of course. That was what had obviously prompted his last move. He didn't credit her with having any principles either, for he only judged by what he knew of her. While admitting bleakly that this was more her fault than his, Helen was conscious there were things she couldn't tell him now. He would simply feel a fool, and be angrier than ever if he were to discover at this late hour he had been wrong about her.

Dully Helen realised she had put off too long and was going to have to suffer the consequences of such foolish procrastination. Her heart aching painfully, she didn't know how she was going to bear it. Being engaged to a man like Stein Maddison would involve quite a lot. People would be ringing up, congratulating them, proffering invitations. They might even be expected to give a party to celebrate and she would have to pretend to be radiantly happy. If she had found the situation difficult before, she suspected, from now on, she might find it almost intolerable.

It began sooner than she expected. During the weekend Stein wasted no time in informing the staff of the engagement. In the early hours, when they arrived back from London, he had taken one look at Helen's shadowed eyes and white face and told her to go to bed. He hadn't repeated his demands, as she had dreaded, for a list of her former boy-friends, but in no other way did he appear to have relented. He ordered champagne and told Helen to wear a pretty dress and smile when he made the announcement.

Having to smile and seem happy was, as she had suspected, something of an ordeal. Stein wore a dark suit for the occasion instead of the casual slacks and shirt he often favoured when he wasn't doing anything special, and Helen knew he looked much more relaxed than she did.

After an hour, during which their health was drunk by a delighted staff, they were left alone again. Helen, feeling almost ill with strain, sank with undisguised relief into the nearest chair. 'Thank goodness that's over!' she breathed wearily.

'Don't grouse,' Stein said shortly, staring at her. 'You complained about your lot before, but as my fiancée your presence here can't be criticised. It will be your own fault now if it is.'

'I did my best,' she said flatly.

His mouth curled. 'You're going to convince no one unless you try harder.'

Hurt by his sarcasm, she asked tensely, 'What about your friends, will they expect a party too?'

'A few drinks, perhaps,' he shrugged, his eyes going closely over her.

She read something in his glance which made her uneasy. Her face flushed as his eyes lingered on her slender curves and her pulse began tripping. She could feel the heat racing through her veins and blurted wildly, 'People will start ringing up, maybe calling. Didn't you ever stop to think before you embarked on this crazy engagement?'

'Don't let me hear you call it that again,' he snapped angrily.

'I don't like deceiving people,' she said stubbornly. 'I enjoyed meeting your stepmother . . .'

'Did you?' he cut in curtly, his tone suggesting no one would have guessed it.

Helen tried to hide her hurt. She had been about to ask why he had never told her about Estella before, but changed her mind. He would only reply with a withering remark which she might deserve. Eighteen months ago she had never tried to pretend she was interested in either Stein or his family.

'You know I enjoyed meeting her,' she sighed, 'but she's going to be disappointed when she hears we aren't going to be married. She seems to believe you—that you're fond of me,' she amended hastily, wondering hollowly what Stein would have said if she'd mentioned love.

'She'll get over it,' he assured her smoothly.

'What about all your girl-friends?' Helen was stung to retort. 'Barbara, for instance. How is she going to feel?'

'I'm sure I'll be forgiven,' he smiled tauntingly, 'especially after you disappear for good. She'll enjoy consoling me.'

She would. Bitterly Helen stared at him. 'Don't you mind about breaking hearts?'

Stein laughed cynically. 'Not many hearts actually break.'

She had been thinking mostly of her own. Anger welled in her throat, but she managed to ask levelly, 'How am I supposed to pass the time, until you decide you don't want me any more?'

'How will you pass it when I don't?' he countered, almost idly.

'I'll get a job!' she said impatiently.

'If you're able to.'

'I know it mightn't be easy.'

'It never is—for girls in a certain condition,' he shrugged.

Helen was in shock when she stared at him, her face white. 'You can't be serious!'

'Maybe not,' he rasped contemptuously, 'but you'd deserve it.'

Helen trembled, with a terrible need to be convinced. 'I can't believe that even you would allow a lust for revenge to drive you that far!'

His eyes glittered down on her as he suddenly gripped her neck between his hands. His expression terrified her, as did the pressure of his fingers on her throat. Why did he so often look as if he would like to kill her? Helen felt frozen with fear while her heart threatened to thud out of her body.

'Please,' she reiterated desperately, 'you can't do anything like that to me!'

'It has to be something,' he snapped unrelentingly, 'that you won't forget in a hurry!'

CHAPTER NINE

As though to convince her he wasn't making idle threats, Stein's hands slid to her shoulders, under the loose neckline of her dress, his touch burning her skin. Helen shivered as she responded, as she guessed he had known she would. He was demonstrating how easily he could bend her to his will. She hadn't the strength to defy him and he knew it. Whenever he was near her she became possessed of cravings which might make her ultimate surrender an easy victory for him. Even now while he filled her with apprehension, she was aware of an obsessive desire for the touch of his lips. Briefly she closed her eyes, willing the sensation away.

'If you managed to do that . . .' she breathed.

'Don't doubt it,' he said, the deadly softness of his voice confirming her fears, 'if I wanted to, Helen, I could.'

'If you did,' she had to lick dry lips before she could force herself to go on, 'how would you feel, having a—a child you never saw?'

'I'd adopt it afterwards.'

'I can't believe it,' she gasped, 'but I wouldn't let you.'

'You might not be able to stop me,' his hands tightened on her narrow bones until she winced with pain. 'At least,' he added harshly, 'I'd have a damned good try, and the publicity wouldn't do you much good.'

'Nor you!' she almost sobbed.

'It's different for a man,' he said coolly, 'especially one in my position.'

'You haven't any conscience!' she whispered thickly.

'I've as much as you ever had!' he snarled, nearly throwing her from him.

He spent the rest of the day in the study and the next morning Helen found him on the verge of departing for London as she came downstairs.

He glanced around when he heard her and said casually, 'I'm just off. I'll give you a ring later.'

Helen nodded, feeling sure he had intended leaving without saying goodbye. She was conscious of his prolonged stare, taking in every detail of her face and figure, and was uneasily aware of her own eyes going just as closely over his. If only he wasn't so attractive, she thought despairingly.

As she was examining the firm line of his jaw and the deep cleft in his chin, he spoke again.

'Stay at home. It's a cold day.'

The words seemed dragged out of him, and she wondered why. Did he believe, as soon as his back was turned, she would try and escape?

'I won't go far,' she replied dully.

'I hope I can trust you!' He caught her wrist, startling her by pulling her savagely to him. 'Hilary's coming,' he muttered curtly under his breath. 'Smile at me!'

Helen fought desperately to keep the pain out of her face and obey. She willed herself to stop trembling while Stein watched her with a kind of raw intentness. 'You heard what I said?'

'I am smiling,' she swallowed.

'About going out!' he muttered between his teeth.

Thinly she murmured, 'I haven't any money to go anywhere.'

It was a mistake and she knew it, even before he reached for his wallet. 'So you want more?'

She protested quickly, cursing herself. 'No, I don't. I won't be deeper in your debt.'

'What difference could it make?' he asked cynically.

'A lot to me,' she retorted sharply. 'I'll get a job and earn all I need.'

'You won't!'

Helen shivered, her delicate features taut with strain. 'You'll never trust me again, will you?'

'I haven't time to argue.' He replaced his wallet impatiently with a quick glance at the hall clock. 'I have a full day—too full.'

Hilary had disappeared, but Stein still dropped a hard kiss on Helen's soft mouth before releasing her. 'Just so you won't forget me,' he said mockingly.

She watched him striding through the door, his straight back and broad shoulders impeccably clad in dark blue. He looked what he was, a successful man, from the top of his well-groomed head to the tip of his expensive shoes. Helen could scarcely believe she had ever thought of him as anything else. Paul was waiting for him and as they drove swiftly away Stein didn't glance up. Before the car had gone many yards, Helen saw him take some papers from his briefcase and begin studying them.

She watched until the car was out of sight, the imprint of Stein's kiss still warm on her lips. Nobody in her whole life had ever set out to hurt and humiliate her so, yet she found it impossible to hate him. But he hated her, and, because of his hate, her love must be completely illogical. As was the concern she felt. This morning he had looked tired. There had been shadows under his eyes and the hard bones of his face had seemed to stand out. Something was bothering him, like a thorn in his side, and it gave her no satisfaction to realise it might be herself.

She told Hilary she would just have coffee. Drinking it at the dining-room table, she noticed Stein's empty cup. He couldn't have been hungry, either, as although the coffee pot had been empty, nothing else seemed to have been touched. Helen eyed the full toast rack despondently, nodding absently when Hilary tried to talk. She mentioned rather obviously that Easter was a nice time for weddings.

Hilary, she could tell, was dying to ask when she and Stein intended getting married, but she didn't give her any encouragement. She refused to carry such a game of makebelieve any farther than was absolutely necessary. What would Hilary say if she confessed that Stein, in announcing their engagement, was merely doing his best to prevent gossip until he was through with her? And that marriage was the last thing he had in mind!

Helen felt distraught as she recalled his terrible threats. It was hard to believe he meant everything he had said, but the uncertainty was already having a devastating effect. After a restless night of bad dreams she felt almost ill again. Where she was concerned, Stein's personality seemed to have changed beyond all recognition. No man was a hundred per cent civilised. Hadn't she read somewhere that most men had a primitive streak? Carefully disguised, of course, and usually under control, but ready to flare when provoked, especially in unusual circumstances.

No one could say that circumstances here were anything but unusual! Suppressing a fresh wave of apprehension, Helen bit her lip. If Stein was serious about carrying out his threats, loving him as she did, would she ever be able to resist him? The answer produced by her tortured mind didn't take a lot of believing. Not when it was backed up by recollections of how eagerly her body melted against his whenever he took her in his arms.

She spent the rest of the day wondering how long she could remain at Oakfield, how long she could endure it. On the face of it, being engaged to Stein might have given her a certain status, but it really meant nothing. She hadn't the heart to begin planning for a future that didn't really exist.

Because she couldn't settle to anything, not even to watching TV or reading, which she normally enjoyed, time dragged. She was so restless she almost welcomed hearing Stein's voice when he rang, as he had promised, later in the afternoon. When he told her he wouldn't be home again for at least the next two nights, her heart sank despite her relief. He had no time to talk, he said. What he meant, she realised, was that he didn't want to.

She fretted so much about why he wasn't coming home that the following afternoon when Gary Phillips called, she found herself amazingly pleased to see him.

'Come out for a drink?' he invited her eagerly.

Helen gazed at him uncertainly. Stein had told her not to have anything more to do with him, but she felt desperate. Stein had left her here in circumstances which seemed to have changed her home into a kind of prison. She was rapidly becoming convinced that if she didn't do something soon, or have a change of company, she might go mad. Besides, she thought bitterly, could Gary's intentions be any worse than Stein's?

'You know I'm engaged?' she asked slowly, feeling it was only fair to mention it.

'Yes, I do,' Gary grinned ruefully. 'I've been thinking all morning it's just my luck!'

'All morning?' Helen frowned enquiringly.

'It's in all the papers. Didn't you know?'

Confused, Helen shook her head. 'Stein's away . . .'

Gary nodded. 'Yes, I've just seen him. I was seeing a friend off at Heathrow and he was getting on the same plane, complete with glamorous secretary. I envied him both you and her, I can tell you!'

Helen was so startled she couldn't hide her dismay.

'Didn't he mention it?' Gary asked smoothly.

She recovered herself quickly. 'Stein travels a lot. He probably did tell me and I forgot. I've had so much to think about.'

The last was true, at least, and if Gary didn't believe the rest, he didn't actually say so.

'No wonder he was annoyed when he thought you might be transferring your affections to me,' he laughed. 'I wanted to apologise about that evening, I'm

afraid I didn't show up very well, but when I tried to
ring and speak to you, Stein wouldn't allow it.'

'So that's why you're here today?'

'Partly,' he agreed. 'I asked Beryl to come, but I
think she's still rather put out that you gave us no hint.'

Helen shrugged, thinking it might be better to let this
pass, rather than confess that she couldn't have done, as
she hadn't known then herself.

'I'm only asking you out for a drink,' Gary smiled as
she frowned, 'I promise to behave myself.'

Still feeling too nervous of Stein to accept, Helen
decided to ask him in for one. Suddenly she welcomed
anything or anyone who might help her to pass an hour
or two, and she didn't believe Stein could object to that.

Surprisingly Gary seemed to quite like the idea of
spending a lazy afternoon before the fire, and
eventually he stayed for tea. His company did prove a
diversion and Helen felt warmly grateful as she saw him
out. She was unable to tell him so, of course, as she was
supposed to be a happily engaged girl. When he
suddenly grabbed her and kissed her, as he was saying
goodbye, she was briefly alarmed, but her gratitude was
such that she recklessly kissed him in return.

It was only a light kiss and she was defiant rather
than frightened as the door closed behind Gary and she
turned to find Mrs Swinden watching her from the back
of the hall. She still didn't care that much for Mrs
Swinden, although the woman was a lot more pleasant
than she had been. Helen, not usually vindictive, didn't
see why she should deny herself a little revenge. Owing
to her changed status, Mrs Swinden wouldn't dare
mention to Stein that Gary had been here, and having
to keep the information to herself might prove painfully
frustrating!

The therapeutic effect of Gary's visit might have been
good while it lasted, but as soon as he had gone Helen
began thinking of Stein again. Going to her room, she
flung herself miserably on her bed. Why hadn't he told

her he was going abroad? And who had he been with? Mrs Wilkinson would never have caught Gary's eye. Had it been Barbara Bates? Helen wondered unhappily. She buried her face in her hands, realising it was futile to conjecture. It might have been anybody. Barbara would only be one of the many women Stein knew. And, whoever it was, she had no right to complain as he was, after all, a free agent. He had never pretended their engagement was real or that he loved her. It might even be better if he had fallen for another woman, Helen tried to persuade herself, then he might be willing to release her.

Wearily she showered and went down to dinner. She was gazing with uninterest at the soup Hilary had set before her when the dining-room door opened and Mrs Swinden showed Donald Blyth in.

If Helen had been surprised to see Gary Phillips, she was stunned when Donald walked in. She stared at him, her blue eyes dark with alarm, while feeling furious with Mrs Swinden. If Stein had been here, the housekeeper would never have dared do such a thing. Helen wondered wildly what she thought she was playing at.

'I'm in the middle of my dinner,' she said coldly, and, she thought, unnecessarily.

Mrs Swinden cut in, just as Helen was about to ask her to take Mr Blyth out again. 'Mr Blyth did say he was a very old friend.'

'A hungry one too,' Donald grinned.

'As Mr Maddison won't be home tonight, there's plenty to spare,' Mrs Swinden assured her hurriedly.

Helen glared, dismissing her. As Mrs Swinden quickly departed, she turned her full attention on Donald. Why had he come here? Stein had been right to warn her. 'You may have forced your way in,' she said furiously, 'but you can't stay!'

He had the nerve to pull out a chair near her and sink into it. 'Have a heart, Helen!' he groaned. 'I only want a word with you, I swear.' Wearily he pushed a hand through his rumpled hair. 'I'd like to know what's going on. It's been like a conspiracy. The man in your lodge wrongly directed me twice. I must have been half way round the entire South of England!'

Unimpressed, Helen stared at him mutely. It didn't seem possible, but he began hungrily eating a roll. He looked ruffled and pale but quite immovable. 'I should get one of the other men to throw you out,' she said crossly.

'You wouldn't be so cruel, darling,' he pleaded, then, hastily, as her eyes flashed as he called her darling, 'I know what you're thinking, but I promise I'm not after news.'

'Which is just as well,' she snapped, 'because you aren't getting any.'

He smiled wryly. 'You used to be such a quiet little thing . . .'

She had been—quiet and reserved. Underneath she still was, but she didn't want Donald to know that. The cloak of confidence she sometimes managed to assume was merely a residue from the days when a touch of it had persuaded her father that she might yet make a good substitute for a son.

'In those days you had no wish to plaster my name all over your paper!' she said severely.

His brows rose ruefully. 'Why can't I convince you it's nothing like that I've come to see you about? Do you think I'd risk running foul of Stein Maddison for the sake of a few lines in a gossip column? I had to see you again to make sure I hadn't a chance.'

Hilary brought him in some soup and as she went out again, Helen frowned. 'A chance?'

'Sure,' his face darkened and he surprisingly ignored the soup. 'You mightn't realise it, Helen, but I love you.'

'Once you thought you did,' she corrected dryly.

'I did!' he insisted, 'but you didn't want me. I thought I'd got over you, though, until I saw you again, then it all came back. It hit me that night like an avalanche. That's why I have to be sure you aren't making a mistake over Maddison.'

Helen laughed hollowly at that. She had made more mistakes over Stein than she cared to remember, but they weren't the kind of mistakes Donald was talking of. She loved Stein, there was no mistake about that—unhappily she wished there had been.

Before she looked away from Donald, her face must have betrayed her. 'So I am too late,' he breathed. 'You've fallen for him?'

'Yes,' she whispered, knowing it would be futile to deny it. Donald was trained to see under the surface, she could never hope to fool him completely. What he didn't realise, and what she could never tell him, was that she derived a strange and maybe unkind comfort from knowing someone else was as miserable.

Donald went a shade paler and muttered something, but to Helen's relief began eating his soup. She doubted if his heart would be past mending, but she let him finish his dinner before requesting him again to leave. He went reluctantly, but this time he didn't argue, and when he had gone Helen went to bed, thinking it had been a bewildering day. Donald had looked pretty grim as he'd left, and she hadn't known whether to feel sorrier for him or herself. Stein might murder her if he was ever to discover Donald had been here. She could only hope again that a fear of offending the girl she must believe to be her future mistress might prevent Mrs Swinden from mentioning either of her two visitors to him.

At eleven the following morning, Helen was just setting off for a walk when Hilary ran after her. Mrs Swinden had sent her to say there was a call for her from France.

To Helen's surprise it was Raissa Sibour, now Madame Gabriel. 'It's wonderful to speak to you again, *chérie*,' the Frenchwoman cried. 'You must tell me how you have been.'

After Helen had replied haltingly that she was well, and in turn enquired about Raissa and her family, there was a slight pause before Raissa asked, 'You wouldn't consider coming back to us, *chérie*? My mother is really too old to be of much practical help and the children have never been as good since you left. We did get another girl, but she isn't nearly as efficient.'

Helen almost accepted eagerly as she thought she saw an immediate way out of her troubles. Then she realised she couldn't She still owed Stein too much—even if the repayment of her debts was becoming harder. She found it difficult, however, to reject her friend's plea out of hand and promised to think it over. If only there was a way! she thought despondently. Without Stein she would never be happy but wouldn't anything be better than having to live with him, being constantly bruised by his hate and distrust?

It was late in the afternoon when he got in touch with her, and despite everything a tremor of joy ran through her on hearing his voice. She was still pondering over Raissa's call when the phone rang and she forgot everything else.

'So you're back!' she exclaimed without thinking, and could have bitten her tongue off at his obvious surprise.

'Back from where?' he asked suavely.

'Just a—a joke,' she tried to laugh, hoping he would treat it as such.

He appeared to, although there was no hint that he was amused. He might have been tired, because he sounded impatient. 'Listen, Helen. Some of the staff from your father's old firm are giving a small party for us this evening. Just drinks and that sort of thing, and Paul's on his way to pick you up.'

He rang off without giving her a chance to comment, and she stared with indignant misery at the buzzing receiver in her hands. She was getting sick of such high-handedness, she told herself bitterly, very sick indeed!

When Paul arrived she was ready. In spite of her rebellious mood she was glad to break the routine of the past few days. Nothing, she decided, could be much worse than having nothing to do. She didn't feel too happy about deceiving her father's old colleagues, many of whom had taken a great interest in her. But it was futile wishing, at this late hour, that Stein might have tried to put the party off. As he hadn't, she would just have to make the best of it.

She wore a blue dress and black high-heeled sandals which flattered her small feet and slender legs. The dress, a compromise between day and evening, was beguilingly composed of silk and lace. Through the cunningly fashioned bodice, her skin gleamed with a creamy whiteness which was very attractive. Yet, glancing at herself in the mirror as she brushed her long, shining hair, she suddenly frowned. She knew her figure was good, but she didn't want Stein to think she was deliberately showing it off. She sighed; why worry about what Stein would think when he probably wouldn't notice anyway!

Paul took her straight to the old works. 'I'm starting here on Monday,' he surprised her by stating as they arrived. 'Mr Maddison found me something.'

Another possible ally gone! 'What if you don't like it?' Helen asked soberly.

'Then he'll find me something else,' Paul grinned. 'He's in just about everything, you know. There's plenty to choose from, if I have patience.'

Stein was waiting for her. She had hoped to have a word with him before going to the conference room where Paul told her the party was to be held, but she was disappointed to find he had gone on ahead, although he did come immediately to her side when he saw her.

The brush of his mouth on her lips made her tremble as usual, but his hand steadied her. He lifted his head to allow his eyes to glint over her. 'Very nice!' he said sardonically, moments before they were surrounded.

Much later, just as they were about to leave, he was called to the telephone, and when he returned Helen was apprehensively startled by the brief glimpse of something she caught in his eyes. It was gone so quickly she thought she must have imagined it, and did in fact forget all about it as he laughingly caught hold of her around the waist, amid renewed cheers, to guide her outside.

'Everyone was so nice,' she whispered, near to tears as he helped her into his car and they drove from the huge complex.

'Yes,' he said expressionlessly.

'Where's Paul?' She suddenly realised he wasn't with them.

'I've given him a few hours off,' Stein replied smoothly. 'I told him to come to the apartment about ten.' While she was digesting this, he added softly, 'How have you found it at Oakfield while I've been away? Quiet?'

'Yes,' she mumbled, praying he wouldn't notice the increase of colour in her cheeks, 'very.'

The windscreen wipers swished hypnotically while street lamps shone on shiny wet roads. Despite the rest of the traffic, the rain seemed to isolate them in an uneasy silence.

At last Stein asked idly, 'Haven't you had any visitors?'

His voice was so casual, Helen was deceived into believing he was concentrating on his driving and merely making polite conversation. It was only as she hesitated and he repeated his query that her glance flew in undisguised alarm to his face. She was suddenly convinced he knew she had had visitors, and who they had been.

Her mind in a sort of chaos, she tried to think straight. That phone call at the party, the brief glimpse of his expression afterwards. The call must have been from Mrs Swinden, although that puzzled her, for she hadn't told the woman where she was going. Then she remembered something and her face paled. Paul had been in the kitchen waiting for her. He had come from there as she had run downstairs. In all probability he had mentioned where she was going. He wouldn't have thought there was any need for secrecy.

Her worst fears were realised when Stein snapped furiously, 'I'm glad you aren't attempting to go on lying to me, Helen.'

Shock shook her and she flinched but tried to speak steadily. 'Two people called, Stein, but I'd no idea they were coming.'

'Hadn't you?' he said grimly.

'No, I had not!' she retorted angrily, yet trying instinctively to appeal to him. 'I wouldn't have asked them. I don't even like either of them very much.'

'Which I suppose explains why you allowed them to stay as long as they did?'

'Mrs Swinden has been busy!' she exclaimed bitterly.

'Don't try to say she didn't tell me the truth.'

'You must know how she twists it!' Helen said desperately.

'You gave the game away yourself,' he snapped. 'Mrs Swinden merely verified what I'd already suspected.' As the car dipped suicidally into the underground park below his apartment, he added savagely, 'You knew I'd been out of the country, because Phillips told you. I saw him at the airport and he saw me.'

'Yes, he did!' she said sharply, wanting to make sure Stein realised she knew he had been with another woman.

He smiled suddenly, a jeer of diabolical triumph. 'Jealous, were you? Of a mere acquaintance?'

'No!' she insisted too feverishly, as the lift shot upwards and he propelled her ruthlessly into his flat. As the door closed behind them she was immediately conscious of being completely alone with him. An inexplicable panic rose inside her and she tried to calm herself. 'Aren't we going out for dinner?'

'Sorry.' His eyes were cold and gleamed angrily, his jeering humour forgotten. 'We can eat here if you're hungry, but not until you've explained a few things. Make yourself comfortable while I perk some coffee. Then we can talk.'

As he disappeared Helen shrugged out of her velvet cloak and sat down. She wondered why she had mentioned dinner when she didn't even feel like coffee. She tried to relax, but found it impossible. She knew what sort of questions Stein was going to ask and recognising the filthy mood he was in she realised he was going to demand answers. But where was she going to find them? Hadn't he already as much as stated he didn't believe she hadn't arranged to meet Donald Blyth? There was no way she could produce indisputable proof that Donald's arrival at Oakfield had been totally unexpected. Somehow she didn't think Stein would be so angry about Gary Phillips, but she was never sure how he would react.

He returned with the coffee and poured it out. He took so long over it that she felt like screaming, until she realised he was being deliberately slow. He knew she was keyed up and was cruelly testing the strength of her nerves.

He drank half his own coffee in a few impatient gulps, then pushed the tray aside, which made Helen wonder why he had bothered in the first place. Before she had practically touched hers he grabbed her cup, putting it out of the way too.

'What is this?' she demanded, her control nearly breaking as his devious change of tactics confused her.

His glance went insolently over her, probing the lace which covered her slender shoulders. She could see the anger still in him and her heart sank.

'Can't you guess?' he said softly. 'I thought you would have. I want to know why you asked both

Phillips and Blyth to visit you as soon as my back was turned. It was no accident, was it?' His quiet tones turned icy with fury. 'You had it all arranged.'

Helen went pale and stared back at him. 'I didn't . . .'

'Shut up!' he snapped between his teeth. 'Even the servants knew what was going on.'

'You mean your hired spy thinks she does!' Helen choked contemptuously. 'You must know Mrs Swinden hates me. I believe she would stop at nothing to blacken my character!'

'You do that yourself,' he said unpleasantly. 'Two men in one afternoon—and you think you're too good for me!'

Helen drew back with a harsh gasp, suddenly seeing how livid he was. 'You must be out of your mind,' she whispered, 'to say such things!'

His face was masklike and rigid. 'I could be,' he taunted, 'but I'll enjoy making you suffer.'

She shook her head wildly, her eyes wide with fear. She could feel the menace in him, but worse than that she could feel every pulse in her body responding, which frightened her even more. With words she might have a hope of fighting him, but her traitorous body was quick to hint that if he began making love to her she wouldn't stand a chance!

She tried to get up, but Stein immediately caught her, his arms pinning her to the couch. Dizzily she wished she had had the sense to sit elsewhere, but he had looked so contemptuous she had thought he wouldn't come near her.

He held her ruthlessly, his eyes staring into hers, letting her see his hate until the room began to sway.

'I was beginning to trust you,' he said harshly, castigating her with his gaze, 'but you won't make a fool of me again!'

Trembling, Helen twisted, but her struggles were fruitless, the pressure of his body not relaxing an inch. 'I never tried to make a fool of you!' she pleaded entreatingly. 'I know I've done wrong, but not wrong like that.'

His smile was cruel. 'I may have been hooked, but a fish doesn't swallow the same line twice.'

'I'm telling the truth!' She shivered as his strong, hard face convulsed with rage. 'I—I've never belonged to Gary Phillips or Donald Blyth or any other man.'

'Tell that to the Marines!' he sneered, his grey eyes molten. 'Remember, darling, I know what both Phillips and Blyth are. Certainly not types to be interested in innocent little virgins.'

Helen's cheeks went scarlet. 'I don't give a damn what you think!'

Her sudden defiance was foolish. She saw it immediately and closed her eyes against the violent fury in his face.

'You're going to!' he muttered, gritting his teeth. 'Before this night's out you'll be crawling to me on your hands and knees.'

Helen got her hands between them, trying to push him away, but she only came against a solid wall of immovable flesh. Panic-stricken, as his arms tightened, she couldn't extricate herself from the intimacy of his embrace. She could only lie panting against him, watching helplessly as his eyes flickered over her. There was something in his expression which sent terror racing to each one of her nerve ends.

He must have drunk too much at the party, she thought, forgetting he had imbibed very little. If he'd been sober he wouldn't have got in such a rage. She could feel it just now, burning in him, fuelled by an icy determination. He had always meant to make her suffer, and all the signs were that he intended waiting no longer.

'I said I'd wait until you begged,' he gasped, as if he could read her thoughts and was merely adding to them, 'I said I wouldn't take you until then because I was greedy. I wanted your mind as well as your body, but who needs a mercenary little mind like yours? Donald Blyth might be willing to pay for the privilege, but I've already paid. So what the hell am I waiting for?'

His mouth came down savagely, parting her trembling lips, taking them in brutal possession. She sensed his predatory anger was far from appeased. She could hear it in the thudding beat of his heart and feel it in the pressure his arms exerted on her. Her whole body began trembling as his mouth explored hers hotly, and she lay shaking, silently fighting the effect he was having.

The intensity of her own reactions took her by surprise. As Stein continued kissing her and his hands began moving slowly over her, her heartbeats quickened and she felt herself beginning to weaken. Sharp stabs of a strange excitement were shooting through her and every principle she had ever known and clung to was abysmally forgotten. When she struggled to break free of the burning passivity beginning to control her limbs, he defeated the feeble thread of purpose in her mind simply by increasing the pressure and subtle probing of his lips.

His hands lingered on her shoulders, then, with an impatient rasp of breath, he eased her forward and slid down her zip. Grasping the silky material, he removed her dress expertly, flinging it to the floor. The room was warm and when she shivered it was not from cold, Sensation was rushing through her as his hands returned to stroke her near-naked body, threatening to drive her crazy.

'No wonder Blyth braved my lodge-keeper twice,' Stein muttered thickly, 'if this was the kind of welcome he had to look forward to!'

Helen lifted heavy lashes and saw his dark face bending over her, a hot flame in his eyes. 'He's never even kissed me!'

Roughly he said, 'You like to make every man feel

he's the only one who's ever been near you.'

She rubbed her knuckles into suddenly wet eyes, like a child. 'You're the only one who's ever been this close.'

He stared at her, his face white. 'What do you take me for, a gullible fool? Do you think I've forgotten rescuing you once, not far from here?'

Mutely she shook her head. 'But you came in time.'

'I wasn't there every time.'

Helen closed her eyes so she didn't have to watch him despising her. She felt exhausted by his sharp contempt, yet the tension inside her was building up unbearably. She murmured his name passionately, thinking she might go insane if she couldn't say it. Winding her arms tightly round his neck, she whispered it breathlessly against his mouth. 'Stein—Stein . . .!'

His mouth came down hard and she heard his gasping mutter. 'Are you trying to drive me out of my mind?' His lips touched hers in such sensual hunger it inflamed her senses until she groaned. His hands disposed of her bra, then caressed her breasts until his mouth slid down to join them. She gasped at the savagery with which he kissed her, but she couldn't withstand his silent demand for her surrender. When his mouth returned to hers she began kissing him back, if not as expertly, as passionately, until their bodies were writhing and twisting together.

'I want you!' Stein groaned, his voice hoarse as he suddenly picked her up and carried her through to his bedroom. 'I want you,' he repeated thickly, 'and I mean to show you how much!'

CHAPTER TEN

IN his room he lowered her on to the bed, stripping off his shirt as he followed. Briefly Helen was terrified as his hard body came down over hers, but his powerful thighs soon mastered her struggles.

He took her face and stared into her dazed blue eyes. 'You little bitch! I'm going to have you whether you enjoy it or not. Fight me and I promise I'll hurt you!'

For a moment Helen shivered with anguish, but the next she was surrendering blindly as the naked desired in his eyes sent a thousand pulses drumming through her. Harshly his mouth swooped on her swollen pink lips, driving her senses into turmoil. Scarcely conscious of what she was doing, she ran trembling fingertips along his broad back, feeling the muscles contract as she touched him. As he bent to kiss her breasts again, she whimpered and pressed her mouth feverishly to the warm skin of his shoulder, trying to make him understand that she wanted him as fiercely as he wanted her.

She felt suddenly completely without shame about wanting him so much, and no longer did she even attempt to hold back from the hot, pulsing kisses they exchanged. When Stein thrust his strong legs between hers, she lay suppliant beneath him, not wanting to fight him any more, ready to give him everything he demanded. A wave of nervousness made her instinctively quiver, but, as his hardness began to penetrate, he controlled her expertly and she lost all real awareness of what she was doing.

She could feel him moving against her, the thick rasp of his breathing assaulting her ears as his hands curved from her breasts to her hips, pulling her closer up to him. Her senses were reeling from the pressure he was putting on her. Her whole body seemed on fire as the desire he was arousing mounted inside her, consuming even her ability to think. Hearing him gasp hoarsely, she moaned against his ruthless mouth, 'I'm yours, Stein darling, if you want me. I always have been . . .'

He stiffened, his body going rigid. She felt the sudden anger and tension in him descending on her like a mighty weight. There was frightening pain as he savagely imposed himself on her, but as swiftly, the hard, hot pressure of his body and mouth disappeared. She couldn't tell the exact moment, because she thought she must have fainted.

When she came round she had no clear recollection of what had happened. It was daylight, and while she was still in bed Stein was up and dressed, standing beside her, holding a cup of tea. He was observing her coldly, without expression, and she wondered how long he had been there.

While he was pale there was no indication that he was unduly disturbed. 'You'd better drink this,' he advised in cool, controlled tones, as she gazed blankly up at him. 'I'm off to work. After you're dressed, Paul's waiting to take you home. I'll see you there this evening.'

Before she could reply he spun on his heel and was gone, leaving her with only a hazy impression of burning eyes set in a grim face.

Helen lay where she was, frozen with as yet unexamined thoughts. The more she tried to remember the more desperate her despair grew, as the one thing she seemed able to recall with any clarity was her own total abandonment. Her face flushed with shame as she remembered how easily Stein had reduced her to a begging, abject creature without pride and then rejected her. He had looked at her this morning with contempt and she knew she couldn't face him again. Nor Paul! Paul must have spent the night here, there were other bedrooms. What must he be thinking?

Hearing the muffled sound of voices in the hall, she guessed Stein was leaving. As soon as he had gone she stumbled out of bed and began to dress. She was thankful that Stein had brought in her clothes, but her cheeks burned as she wondered if he had managed to do so before Paul had seen them scattered over the lounge.

Money was going to be a problem, the few pounds she had wouldn't take her very far. She had made up her mind she would go to France and work for Raissa, but her biggest difficulty might be getting there.

Stein must have left her to sleep in his room. The other side of the bed was undisturbed, but it was obviously his bedroom she was in. There were odd things, a book by a writer she knew was his favourite, one of his short towelling robes behind the door. She noticed a framed snapshot by the bed and picked it up, startled to see her own face staring back at her. It was one she had had taken almost three years ago—she wondered dully how Stein had come by it.

Replacing it, with hands that trembled from the regret in her heart, she stumbled to the dressing-table to comb her hair. It was here that she found, unexpectedly, a roll of notes, a hundred pounds' worth in all. Briefly thinking it was like an answer to an unconscious prayer, she stuffed them in her handbag. It wasn't stealing, she assured herself feverishly. As soon as she reached France she would begin paying Stein back—this and every other penny she owed.

Quietly she crept into the hall. From the kitchen she heard the sound of a radio turned low, mingling with the occasional clatter of dishes and cutlery. Paul was either eating his breakfast or busy washing up. Swiftly, making no noise, Helen opened the front door and let herself out. Paul would imagine she was still asleep. With any luck, it could be another hour before he went to investigate, and by then she should be well away.

In a second-hand shop several streets away, she exchanged the clothes she was wearing for a pair of jeans and a jacket with a warm sweater to go underneath. It was nearly Easter and it would be warmer in France than it was here, but she had to get there first. She managed to persuade the owner of the shop to provide her with a rucksack too, knowing her cloak alone was worth more than all the rest of the things she had got put together.

Outside the shop she paused, wondering how she should travel. While it might not cost so much to go to France by sea ferry, it would take longer. She was trying to decide whether to ring the airports to see if she could get a flight, or go personally on the offchance of getting one, when she suddenly knew she had to have more time before making a definite decision. She felt so mixed up and unhappy she didn't think it would be fair to either Raissa or her family to descend on them in such a state. And, underlying all her doubts, was a growing reluctance to spend any of Stein's money, even on the fare.

Eventually she decided to make for Newhaven, which she had once visited. She could always get the ferry from there to Dieppe if she changed her mind about going to France. If not, then Newhaven was a busy, popular resort where she might be lucky enough to find work.

She hitch-hiked most of the way, feeling it would be an unnecessary extravagance to travel by bus or train when she had all day and nothing else to do. It did take almost all day. It was early evening when she arrived and began looking round for a place to stay. It had to be somewhere cheap and not conspicuous. If there was a Y.W.C.A. or Youth Hostel, she didn't try and find them, suspecting these could be the first places Stein might look for if by some improbable chance he discovered the direction she had taken. She didn't think she would ever see him again, nor did she want to, but if he was still motivated by a thirst for revenge, he might stop at nothing to find her.

Unfortunately all the boarding houses she tried which looked as if they might accommodate her reasonably were either closed or fully booked for Easter. She had almost given up and was thinking of finding a quiet spot on the promenade as she tried one last place. There seemed to be no one at home, but, after she had knocked twice, the door was eventually opened by a pleasant-looking middle-aged woman.

Helen thought she was in luck until the woman shook her head and ruefully held up a bandaged hand. 'You're the third party I've turned away in the last hour,' she sighed. 'I cut myself badly and can't manage the cooking, you see. The neighbours are good, but they have their own problems.'

Helen said she was sorry and was just about to leave when she was struck by inspiration. She hesitated, then took the plunge nervously. 'I—I don't suppose you'd let me stay and help, until you're better? I'd cook and do anything just for my keep, for a few days.'

The woman gazed at her doubtfully, not deceived by the roughness of Helen's junk-shop attire. 'You somehow seem above that kind of thing,' she said at last.

Helen smiled wryly, hastening to assure her, 'I recently looked after three children in France. I was there for a year, helping with everything—cooking, housework, the lot.'

The woman laughed. 'I must say I think I could come to like you, and it's the first time anyone's ever made me such an offer. Well, I couldn't expect it, could I? I mean we've all got to live, haven't we? I'd be grateful, mind you, if you'd really like to help, but I'm a widow and I'm afraid I can't afford proper wages.'

Helen smiled with relief and said it didn't matter. 'I won't let you down,' she promised.

The woman smiled too, holding open the door.

'Come in then,' she invited warmly, 'You're very welcome, for as long as you care to stay.'

Helen stayed a week before deciding she couldn't go to France but must return to Oakfield. In a way she was reluctant to leave Newhaven as she got on so well with Mrs Lamb, but she couldn't sleep at nights for thinking of Stein. The money she had borrowed was burning a hole in her conscience, as was everything else she owed him. Her love for him, too, was eating her up until she couldn't think straight. She realised one night that she had to see him again and remain with him—if this was what he wanted, regardless of the consequences, until she had settled her debts. Even though his hate might hurt excruciatingly, she had to face it. Running away had solved none of her problems. It had merely labelled her, in her own eyes, at least, as a coward!

Mrs Lamb's hand was better and she was so grateful for everything Helen had done she insisted on giving her five pounds when she left. She made Helen promise that if she was ever in Newhaven again she would come and see her. Helen had told her, quite truthfully but without going into details, that she had been unhappy at home but felt the time had come when she must go back and sort something out. As she said goodbye, she firmly replaced the five pounds in Mrs Lamb's hand, saying gently, and meaning it, that she owed Mrs Lamb much more than Mrs Lamb owed her!

She started off early in the morning, but it was almost dark before she reached Oakfield, which lay fifty miles on the other side of London. As she walked wearily up the drive she almost turned and went away again. She loved Stein and wasn't ashamed of it—if she was ashamed of anything it was that it had taken her so long to realise it, but she wondered if the words she had whispered to him in his bedroom had completely betrayed her. What had she said, in that mindless moment of yearning for a culmination which had never arrived? She remembered murmuring that she had always belonged to him, or something like that. A statement from which Stein's astute brain might easily have extracted the precise meaning. And while she felt she might somehow find the strength to withstand the ridicule he would undoubtedly pour on her head because of other things, she wasn't sure if she would be able to endure it if he began taunting her because of her love for him.

The house looked the same. Around the last bend of the drive Helen paused to gaze at it, a lump in her throat, feeling she might have been away for years instead of days. It was an old house with a warm, graceful appearance which even a cold night like this failed to dim. She had always loved it, but for the second time in her life she felt apprehensive on approaching it.

A dampness touching her face made her realise it was raining and if she hung about much longer she would only get wet. There could be no escaping the ordeal ahead, and the longer she hesitated the faster her courage was ebbing.

The door wasn't locked and she didn't knock. Pushing it open, she walked straight in, fearing the slightest pause might be enough to send her flying back down the drive again.

There was no one around, which wasn't so unusual, but the silence struck Helen as distinctly odd. A kind of shiver ran down her spine as without thinking she dropped her rucksack to the hard polished floor. The ensuing clatter of the metal-ended fasteners echoed in an exaggerated fashion, like a noise in an empty house, and suddenly, as if it really had been quite loud, the study door was flung wide open and Stein stood there.

For all she had come specially to see him, Helen's first instinct was to run. But she had done too much of that already and her legs seemed somehow to have lost their strength. It was the sight of his face, more than anything, which frightened her. It was gaunt, the bones

standing out as if he had lost weight. She noticed the
signs of fatigue about his startled grey eyes and the deep
lines which curved his harshly held mouth. He looked
older, yet it was merely a week since she had seen him.
Surely such a change couldn't be entirely due to her? He
couldn't hate her that much, surely!

'Stein!' she whispered, not realising how pale her own
face was. 'I've come back . . .'

'You have?' The words were rapped out roughly,
Helen felt their impact like a blow.

'I wanted to return the money I borrowed from your
dressing-table.' Quickly she took it from her pocket and
laid it on the hallstand. 'I forgot to leave a note and I
suddenly realised you might think Paul had taken it.'

Brusquely, Stein retorted, 'I don't even recall leaving
it there. I had more important things to think of.' He
advanced towards her with such coldness that she was
immediately terrified.

Blindly she turned, making for the stairs, but she had
barely reached the first step before he caught her. 'My
God, Helen,' he bit out hoarsely, 'what do you think
you're trying to do to me?' With a savage movement he
put a stop to her wild flight. 'Where the devil have you
been?'

He sounded infuriated, almost beyond knowing what
he was saying. Mute with shock, she could only shake
her head.

'You think it's your mission in life to see me suffer?'
he snarled.

His face was icy and barbaric. Helen stared at him as
he spun her fully round to face him, his eyes
annihilating her. 'Stein?' she breathed weakly, as he
forced her to look at him. She wasn't sure what to make
of his livid accusation, but she was astonished at the
driven anger in his face.

'I shouldn't have run away,' she faltered, trying to
hold herself stiffly, so he wouldn't know she was
trembling.

For an answer he drew a deep breath between his teeth and snatching her up in his arms, carried her straight to his study. As she was held tightly against him, her heartbeats quickened, threatening to choke her. She tried desperately to hang on to her deserting senses. What's Mrs Swinden going to think? she wondered distractedly, remembering how the woman rarely missed a thing.

The door closed behind them, but he didn't put her down. Gazing up at him, Helen heard herself confessing helplessly, 'I didn't mean to come back, Stein.'

His eyes flared darkly, lit by a brilliant fury. 'I would have found you. I haven't stopped looking, day or night. God, I could kill you!'

She thought he meant to try, as his mouth descended on hers, taking her breath away. With a smothered groan he dropped her to her feet without allowing her to move from him. He kept her savagely a prisoner, his arms tightening around her as the pressure of his mouth both hurt and exalted her, bringing her to a shuddering realisation of the depth of her feelings for him.

Thrusting a hand through her hair, he twisted it cruelly, not pausing until she whimpered with pain. 'I'll make you suffer!' he muttered roughly. 'Not as much as you've made me—that would be impossible, but I'll make your life a constant misery!'

As she struggled for breath, he spoke hoarsely against her mouth in a voice she scarcely recognised. His lips were hard, taking hers by storm, arousing a storm of wild sensation. Fever began burning along her veins like a scorching fire while every nerve in her body seemed to be leaping. Blindly her arms wound round his neck as she found herself kissing him back, returning passion for passion. What did it matter if he hated her when he could make her feel like this? For a second she was pierced with anguish, until the driving desire in his hands and mouth began changing her sadness to delight.

A shaft of sanity got through as his frenzied kisses eventually had to ease, but when she tried to twist away he placed a hand under her chin, holding her quite still, refusing to let her go.

'I need this,' he muttered thickly, his eyes glazed. 'Don't try and stop me.'

Helen didn't want to. She was ready to give him anything he asked. She had returned to pay, and keep on paying. It was the increasing force of her own emotions that made her terribly afraid. She looked at Stein, her blue eyes wide and feverish, full of uncertainty. 'Please,' she whispered, 'won't you let me explain?'

He laughed harshly, his eyes blazing. 'Do you know what these last few days have done to me? You've killed me by inches, over and over again!'

'Stein?' She was shaking because of his tortured expression, but she had to try and get through to him.

'Where have you been?' He refused to let her speak, nor did he make any attempt to disguise the savage jealousy in his voice as he ruthlessly removed her shabby jacket. 'Dressed like this, like a little tramp! Have you been sleeping in the gutter? And who with?'

'No!' she gasped, suddenly suspecting that his mind might be in an even more unbalanced state than her own.

His eyes were full of icy sparks as they roamed over her, and she bore the anger of his disapproving stare as he surveyed her shapeless sweater and jeans, as bravely as she could.

'Stein!' she entreated again. 'You have to listen!'

'Shut up!' As if to make sure she did, his mouth roughly renewed its assault on hers, and, in the brief moment before she surrendered to its force, Helen wondered apprehensively if, by disappearing as she had, she had driven him too far. Whatever purgatory he was in, he seemed intent on taking her with him as his arms crushed her to him, the feelings he aroused blinding her to everything but her own needs. His hands explored her body, while the pressure of his mouth increased urgently, and she met his silent demands by clinging to him fiercely while white-hot flames consumed them both. Her senses were swimming. In her ears she could only hear her increased heartbeats and the throbbing of Stein's against her breast. Wildly they pounded together until she was driven almost unconscious by the intensity of the sensation flooding through her. Never, not even on the night responsible for her mad flight, had it been quite like this.

'I love you, Stein,' she heard herself breathing beneath his passionate lips. 'I love you . . .'

He became very still. She recognised this stillness in him, for she had experienced it once before. The muscles of his strong neck became wholly tense against her encircling arms and she could feel his body trembling strangely.

'Helen!' he said hoarsely, pulling her head back, the glitter of his eyes bringing her swiftly to her senses. 'Do you realise what you're saying?'

Helen blinked, becoming suddenly as rigid as a small statue as her eyes dilated before the intensity of his. She had confessed that she loved him, she thought she must have said it a thousand times in fevered murmurings and in her mind, but it was still undeniably the truth. She was unable to deny it, and her blue eyes held a dazed reflection of a mind stripped of any ability to deviate.

'I've been fighting it a long time,' she admitted weakly, 'ever since I first knew you. After I came home, after Dad died, I think I realised then what was happening, but I tried to ignore it. I didn't succeed,' she blinked at him through gathering tears. 'Trying not to love you was like trying to avoid getting wet after being caught miles from shelter in a storm. I was soon overwhelmed. Now you can laugh,' she choked, her slender control breaking when he didn't speak, 'I should think your victory must be almost complete?'

'Don't!' Stein swallowed thickly.

Taking no notice, she rushed on hysterically, her small face strained, 'Don't you think it's funny? Nothing could hurt a girl more than loving a man who can't stand the sight of her. You must have achieved much more than you set out to do and you're probably feeling rather embarrassed by it all. But . . .'

Suddenly, almost painfully, he placed a hand over her shaking mouth, stemming the wild tide. 'Helen!' he groaned, the anger in his expression changing to such rare tenderness that she could only stare at him with damp, bewildered eyes. Gently he pulled her down to the sofa, keeping his arms around her. 'Helen,' he repeated huskily, 'why didn't you tell me you loved me before? I've been nearly driven crazy, loving you, longing for you, searching for you. I saw you murdered, raped, lost, frightened, everything imaginable, until I thought I was going insane!'

'You—you did?' she exclaimed in a daze, her eyes fever bright. How could Stein Maddison, so coolly confident and arrogant, be going insane because of her? Yet, gazing at him closely, she was tempted to believe it. He did have the appearance of a man driven to the brink of temporary madness. She saw it in his eyes and had felt it in the frenzy of his kisses. But if he had been so distracted, why hadn't he been pleased to see her?

'You were so angry when I arrived,' she faltered.

He didn't pretend he didn't know what she was talking about. 'I lost my head,' he said grimly, his face paling as though he was only beginning to realise how much and the knowledge astonished him. When he admitted that he couldn't recall it happening before, Helen didn't disbelieve him.

His arms tightened, but the quality of his strength had changed. No longer was he using it to hurt her. She could feel it now, like a protective cloak, remorseful and comfortingly warm instead of coldly frightening.

'You've no idea,' he muttered thickly against her cheek, 'what your disappearance did to me. When I saw you standing in the hall, looking as if you'd just been away having fun, something snapped. I seemed to forget the ordeal I'd just been through, the agony of being unable to find you, or perhaps the strain of it had proved greater than I'd thought. Suddenly you were there, and all I could think of was hurting you—to compensate for some of the torment. I'm sorry, my darling,' he stared at her with agonised eyes, 'I wouldn't hurt a hair of your head—I love you so.'

He had mentioned loving her, but she hadn't allowed herself to believe it for fear he hadn't really meant it. Now she could no longer doubt the depth of feeling in his eyes and voice. 'If only I'd known,' she whispered breathlessly, 'I would never have run away.'

His eyes darkened, as if even to think of it caused him pain. 'When Paul rang and told me you'd gone, I just about flayed him alive over the phone!'

'It wasn't his fault,' she protested in dismay.

'I know it wasn't,' he said ruefully, 'I apologised later, but you don't know how I felt, learning you had left like that, especially after what had happened the night before.'

'We don't have to talk about it,' she whispered.

'Yes, we have,' he insisted roughly but with something in his voice which took her breath away. 'I intended making love to you. I almost did when I suddenly realised how innocent you were.'

Helen laid quick, loving fingers over his lips while a flush stained her cheeks. 'I'm sorry, Stein, that I'm not more—more experienced.'

'I'm not.' His eyes flared darkly, his body tense. 'At the time, though, it was a shock, after everything I'd said and thought.'

'That was mostly my fault,' she confessed.

'When you fainted,' he went on tautly, 'I felt like death. The next morning I could hardly look you in the face. I didn't go to the office until later, I just drove round trying to think. I called in at the office briefly— that was when Paul caught me. I'd decided to return and beg you to marry me, and I knew we had to talk. I realised if I'd been wrong about one thing, I might easily have been wrong over others. I'd been too angry ever since you left home to go to France to see things clearly, but that morning, sitting in my car, I was suddenly convinced there was a lot you'd been hiding from me.'

'A lot I should have told you,' Helen admitted with a shamed nod. 'Oh, Stein,' she put her arms around him tightly, 'if you were stubborn, so was I, but I wasn't ever as bad as you thought. I felt I'd done wrong and it was better that you should think the worst of me. I'd treated you terribly and neglected my father. It seemed only right that I should pay for it.'

'We should have talked,' he said grimly.

'You did.' Her voice was faintly teasing.

'Why didn't you shut me up?' he groaned harshly. 'In France, when I realised how wrong I'd been about you, I nearly went insane.'

'You've been to France?' Helen's eyes widened incredulously. 'When?'

'After I couldn't find you here,' his mouth tightened, as he recalled the agony of a fruitless search. 'I remembered Mrs Swinden telling me you'd had a call from France, and I thought that was where you must have gone.'

'And?'

'All I found was further proof of how wrong I'd been about you. I went first to your friend Madame Sommier, who appeared to take fright at the sight of me. She gabbled on about meaning to return the money you'd given her, which I gathered was the full amount I had sent you.'

As Helen flushed guiltily, he proceeded thickly, 'From there I managed to trace Madame Sibour, who told me how you'd helped her for a year with the children and everything, after her first husband died. Why didn't you say something, Helen?'

Helen swallowed at the reproach in his voice, the pain in his eyes. 'It wasn't because I really intended deceiving anybody.' Confused, she bent her head. 'The reason began long before I left England. You must know that.'

'I knew things were bad,' Stein agreed tautly, 'but then it had been bad between us, hadn't it, from the very beginning?' As Helen glanced up at him quickly, and hesitated, he insisted gently, 'I think the time has come to be completely honest with each other, darling, if we're to make a fresh start.'

She nodded with a sigh. 'It's just that Dad was a part of it and I wouldn't want it to seem that I was criticising him. I believe he always believed he was acting for the best.'

'Not always with the best results,' Stein interposed grimly.

Helen sighed again. 'When he sold you the factory he made you promise not to tell me, but you obviously didn't understand why that should make me so antagonistic.'

Stein shook his head. 'In the end that was what made me so angry. Was there a special reason, other than that you didn't like me?'

'I thought I didn't like you!' she corrected soberly with a certain wryness in her eyes. 'But yes, it was more than that. You didn't know what had gone before. You see, Dad always regretted that I wasn't a boy. Ever since I can remember he'd pushed me hard. That was what made me frightened of horses. When I was small, one day he threw me on to one and I fell off, with rather dire consequences. He never usually drove me too far, though. I think he recognised that there were limits and was often sorry afterwards. I believe that was why I kept on trying.'

As he listened to Helen's short, rather stilted sentences, Stein's face hardened with anger kept in check. 'And the factory?'

Helen shrugged, attempting to make little of it. She didn't want Stein to hate her father over something which lay in the past. 'I wasn't too keen to begin with,' she admitted, 'but I tried to live up to his expectations. I really felt I might make a go of it when he suddenly said he had you and didn't need me any more. He talked of needing me more at home. I realised why he hadn't wanted me at the works, after Mr Dent told me what had actually happened, but at the time I blamed you.'

A muscle at the side of Stein's mouth jerked and she frowned. 'I wish I could understand why he did it, but I suppose we'll never know.'

Some of the anger died from his grey eyes as he noted the distress Helen was doing her best to hide. 'He loved you, darling, make no mistake about that, but a man's pride can be the very devil. I imagine he'd criticised you so much, he couldn't face the fact that it was he who'd failed.'

'I don't see why you put up with me, though.' She turned troubled eyes to him, 'I was really beastly to you—and in ways you never guessed!'

'Oh,' he smiled laconically, 'I had a good idea.'

'But you couldn't have—have loved me at the beginning,' she stammered, her face pink.

He ran teasing fingers over her hot cheek, easing the tension between them slightly. 'I saw you once,' he confessed, with a hint of self-derision, 'at Heathrow with Lester. I think I fell in love with you on the spot, and I mistakenly fancied my usual luck was with me when I heard, a few days later, that your father was thinking of selling up. It gave me quite a shock, I can tell you, when I began to realise that, as far as you were concerned, nothing was going to be plain sailing. You obviously thought I was a Jake on the make.' He grinned wryly. 'The only response I got was when I kissed you and I was half mad with frustration. Mind you,' he muttered severely, 'don't imagine I intended putting up with it indefinitely. But before I could do anything you ran away.'

'It seemed all I could do, after that last evening, when you rescued me,' Helen confessed, her face strained, despite Stein's thread of humour. 'I knew then you were some kind of threat and I panicked, that's really why I ran. I was beginning to love you and I couldn't endure it, not when I was so determined to dislike you.'

'You stayed in France?'

'I didn't mean to, not as long as I did, but when Raissa's husband died there seemed no one else free to give her the kind of help she needed.'

'And for no charge,' he said grimly.

'Well,' Helen retorted, 'it wasn't as if she didn't offer, or made any attempt to force me. Perhaps I used her just as much, as an excuse for not coming back. The trouble was,' she sighed, 'the longer I stayed the less courage I could find for returning to face you.'

'But you did in the end,' he said softly.

'Yes,' she glanced at him almost shyly. 'Apart from wanting to see Dad, I knew I had a lot to apologise for. I was going to ask you if we could begin again.'

'Oh, my sweet!' he groaned, pulling her closer. 'If only you knew the times I had to forcibly restrain myself from coming to get you! I was still too angry to trust myself not to do you physical harm.' He laughed, again with a hint of self-derision, 'I wonder why I never asked myself why I didn't just simply forget you, instead of allowing you to obsess me?'

'When I did come home,' she sighed tensely, 'I thought I could actually feel you hating me.'

'I thought I did.' His mouth twisted. 'I was in a jealous rage, thinking of you being with another man in Paris, and even more furious when I took one look at you and realised, after a whole bloody year, my love for you was as strong as ever. That was why I believe I was so cruel about your father. Oh, Helen, my love,' he groaned against her cheek, 'I can't tell you how much I've regretted that!'

'I had neglected him, Stein.'

'I don't agree,' Stein retorted. 'He did confess a few things, from time to time, after you'd gone, which make sense in view of what you've just told me. I can understand almost everything now. What I can't is the way I've used you.'

Helen felt so secure and warm from his love that that didn't seem to worry her any more. When he had finished pressing soft, remorseful kisses on her mouth, she managed to murmur teasingly, 'What did you intend doing with me eventually, darling?'

'Marry you,' he rejoined tersely, slipping on her finger her ring which he drew from his pocket. Not sharing her contented smile, he snapped, 'You didn't think our engagement wasn't for real?'

'I wondered if it was for your stepmother's benefit.'

'Estella?' he shrugged broad shoulders. 'I believe I hoped that her knowing would help cement it, but it was really your Mr Phillips who brought things to a head. I suddenly knew I couldn't risk losing you, to him or any other man, and the only way it seemed to prevent that was by announcing to the world you were mine. A few days later, when Mrs Swinden reported that you'd been entertaining both Phillips and Donald Blyth, you might understand why I saw red. That evening, when I returned to the party, I meant to make you crawl, but I paid for it a thousand times over.'

'Oh, Stein,' she breathed, her eyes damp with tears, 'I promise I'll never run away again.'

'You still haven't told me where you've been,' he frowned anxiously, kissing the tears from her wet cheeks.

The way he was kissing her made her weak, but she managed to relate fairly clearly about being uncertain about going back to Raissa, in France, and deciding to go to Newhaven before coming to a definite decision. She told him how she had stayed in Newhaven with Mrs Lamb and what she had done, which evoked from Stein an impatient but loving sigh, after which Helen said nervously, 'I soon knew I had to come back to you. I wasn't sure what kind of reception I'd get, I didn't expect you would forgive me, but I realised I couldn't leave you, not until you threw me out anyway.'

'Why?' he asked huskily, fiercely demanding.

'Because I was aware of how much I loved you,' she said softly, giving him unequivocally the answer he wanted.

'Darling,' he muttered, his voice uneven with passion, 'say that again.' When she obliged, he threatened thickly, 'I'll need to hear it constantly, both day and night. I'll never get tired of hearing it, I love you so much.'

'Won't Mrs Swinden be coming to see what's going on?' Helen murmured much later, when Stein allowed her to speak again. She tried to force a little amusement into her voice, but her flushed face quickly paled.

Her apprehension, however, changed to surprise as Stein reluctantly stopped kissing her and raised his head. 'Mrs Swinden isn't here any more,' he said.

'Not here any more?' Helen's eyes went blank with astonishment. 'You mean she's taken a holiday?'

'No, my love,' he smiled grimly, 'she's taken six months' wages instead of notice, and she's gone for good. I did ask her to report to me if ever you left Oakfield, but I told her that was because you'd been ill and I didn't want you running unnecessary risks. I've discovered since then that she exaggerated almost everything, although I don't absolve myself from all the blame.'

Helen hesitated. 'I don't think she ever liked me, Stein, but I'd hate to think I was responsible for her losing her job.'

'She deserved to,' he said curtly. 'For instance, she lied so much over the length of time Blyth had spent here that when you disappeared my first thought was that you were with him. I'm afraid his flat was the first place I went to. He informed me rather bitterly, in the course of our—er—conversation, that you hadn't invited him anywhere, and if he'd been in my shoes you would never have got away from him. He said he'd been to see you here, but only to ask if he had a chance. He admitted he'd arrived while you were having dinner and Mrs Swinden had offered him some, but you hadn't been pleased to see him and immediately afterwards you'd sent him away. I'm afraid neither of us was very polite.'

Helen could imagine! 'What about Barbara?' she asked suddenly, remembering how the thought of Stein with other women had tormented her. She hadn't meant to ask, but somehow she couldn't prevent herself.

Stein hesitated, but only for a moment. 'Barbara,' he said quietly, 'was your father's friend, not mine. I don't think there was anything very serious, but after Lester died she took a lot of consoling—so much so, that I began to suspect she hoped I'd be willing to replace him. Unfortunately I had no such ambitions. The last time I saw her was that evening she came to the flat uninvited, when you were there. I suppose,' he confessed wryly, 'I was rather abrupt, but I made it plain in as few words as possible that I wasn't interested.'

'I thought I'd offended her.'

Stein smiled slightly and shook his head. 'Haven't I told you there's been no one since I met you? If I ever took another woman out to dinner it never meant more than a quirk of desperate defiance at the hold you appeared to have over me. You've a lot to answer for, you little minx!'

Helen gulped at his threatening growl and decided it might be wiser to concentrate on the servant problem.

'What about Hilary and Olive? They were all right.'

'I gave them a couple of weeks' holiday,' he said, 'until we can find another housekeeper.'

'I don't think we need one,' Helen said firmly, 'And,' she smiled, 'as the girls aren't here, I'll begin proving it to you by cooking your supper.'

'I'll have something to say about that!' Stein exclaimed. 'In the meantime, I suppose we'd better have something before I take you back to London.'

'To London?' Apprehensively she pulled from his arms, cold with dismay.

'Come back here!' he renewed his hold on her sternly, a wicked gleam in his eyes. 'I won't tell you why if you don't behave yourself!'

While Helen took a deep breath, he bent teasingly to her delicate ear. 'We're going to London for my stepmother has returned and you can stay with her until tomorrow—when we'll be married.' The glint of humour died from his expression as he heard Helen's faint gasp and he turned her chin up so he could look deep into her startled eyes. 'You mightn't know it, but I've had a licence burning a hole in my pocket for days.'

'Stein!' she whispered incredulously. 'I can't believe you're serious . . .'

'Tomorrow evening you will,' he assured her gravely in a way that made her heart race. 'There are things you're never going to doubt again.'

The radiance in her eyes almost halted him in his tracks as he began raining kisses on her face. As his mouth grew more demanding and his arms tightened urgently, he murmured huskily against her quivering lips, 'The choice is yours, of course. If we stay here overnight there'll still be a wedding, but I can't guarantee to keep out of your bed. I love you and want you too much, my darling.'

For a moment Helen was tempted, and was aware she had betrayed herself as her cheeks flushed and she heard the rasp of Stein's indrawn breath. Then she thought of how long they had already waited, of all the other nights they would have, and she knew the sacrifice of a few more hours would perhaps make their life together all the more worthwhile.

'We'll go to London,' she replied softly, although she did wonder, as the pressure of Stein's mouth deepened sensuously and the world faded, just how long it might be before they got there.

Harlequin® Plus

A WORD ABOUT THE AUTHOR

Margaret Pargeter's earliest memories are of her child-hood in Northumberland, in northern England. World War II was raging, but in spite of the gravity of the times, she recalls, people always tried to find something to smile about. That memory, and that philosophy, have stayed with her through the years.

Short-story writing was a habit that began in her early teens, and after her marriage she wrote serials for a newspaper. When her children were in school she did several years of market research, which she believes gave her a greater insight about people and their problems, insight that today helps her in creating interesting plots and developing believable characters.

Today, Margaret lives in a small house in the quiet Northumbrian valley where she grew up. On the subject of writing romances, she is convinced of one thing: "It is not easy. But not the least among my blessings is the pleasure I get from knowing that people enjoy reading my books."

HARLEQUIN
PREMIERE AUTHOR EDITIONS

6 top Harlequin authors — 6 of their best book

1. JANET DAILEY Giant of Mesabi

2. CHARLOTTE LAMB Dark Master

3. ROBERTA LEIGH Heart of the Lion

4. ANNE MATHER Legacy of the Past

5. ANNE WEALE Stowaway

6. VIOLET WINSPEAR The Burning Sands

Harlequin is proud to offer these 6 exciting romance novels by 6 of our most popular authors. In brand-new beautifully designed covers, each Harlequin Premiere Author Edition is a bestselling love story—a contemporary, compelling and passionate read to remember!

Available wherever paperback books are sold, *or* through Harlequin Reader Service. Simply complete and mail the coupon below.

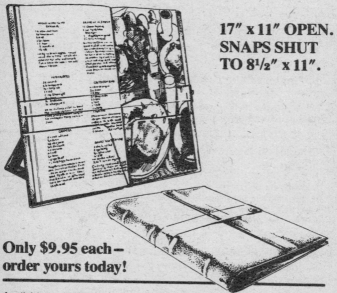

ROBERTA LEIGH

Collector's Edition

A specially designed collection of six exciting love stories by one of the world's favorite romance writers—Roberta Leigh, author of more than 60 bestselling novels!

1 **Love in Store**
2 **Night of Love**
3 **Flower of the Desert**
4 **The Savage Aristocrat**
5 **The Facts of Love**
6 **Too Young to Love**

Available now wherever paperback books are sold, or available through Harlequin Reader Service. Simply complete and mail the coupon below.

Harlequin Reader Service

In the U.S.
P.O. Box 52040
Phoenix, AZ 85072-9988

In Canada
649 Ontario Street
Stratford, Ontario N5A 6W2

Please send me the following editions of the Harlequin Roberta Leigh Collector's Editions. I am enclosing my check or money order for $1.95 for each copy ordered, plus 75¢ to cover postage and handling.

☐ 1   ☐ 2   ☐ 3   ☐ 4   ☐ 5   ☐ 6

Number of books checked_____ @ $1.95 each = $_____

N.Y. state and Ariz. residents add appropriate sales tax $_____

Postage and handling $_____.75____

TOTAL $_____

I enclose_____

(Please send check or money order. We cannot be responsible for cash sent through the mail.) Price subject to change without notice.

NAME_____
(Please Print)

ADDRESS_____ APT. NO._____

CITY_____

STATE/PROV._____ ZIP/POSTAL CODE_____

Offer expires June 30, 1984   31256000000